# The HERO and His ELF BRIDE Open a PIZZA PARLOR in ANOTHER WORLD

## Kaya Kizaki

ILLUSTRATION BY
Shiso

# The HERO and His ELF BRIDE Open a PIZZA PARLOR in ANOTHER WORLD

## Kaya Kizaki

Translation by Kevin Steinbach
Cover art by Shiso

YUSHA DESUGA ISEKAI DE ELF YOME TO PIZZA TEN HAJIMEMASU
© 2017 by Kaya Kizaki, Shiso
All rights reserved.
First published in Japan in 2017 by SHUEISHA, Inc.
English translation rights arranged by SHUEISHA, Inc.
through Tuttle-Mori Agency, Inc., Tokyo.

English translation © 2018 by Yen Press, LLC

Yen On
1290 Avenue of the Americas
New York, NY 10104

Visit us at yenpress.com

facebook.com/yenpress
twitter.com/yenpress
yenpress.tumblr.com
instagram.com/yenpress

First Yen On Edition: November 2018

Yen On is an imprint of Yen Press, LLC.
The Yen On name and logo are trademarks of Yen Press, LLC.

Library of Congress Cataloging-in-Publication Data
Names: Kizaki, Kaya, author. | Shiso, illustrator. | Steinbach, Kevin, translator.
Title: The hero and his elf bride open a pizza parlor in another world / Kaya Kizaki ;
    illustration by Shiso ; translation by Kevin Steinbach.
Other titles: Yusha desuga isekai de elf yome to pizza ten hajimemasu. English
Description: First Yen On edition. | New York, NY : Yen On, November 2018.
Identifiers: LCCN 2018021927 | ISBN 9781975353254 (pbk.)
Subjects: CYAC: Humorous stories. | Fantasy. | Heroes—Fiction. | Pizza—Fiction.
Classification: LCC PZ7.1.K633 He 2018 | DDC [Fic]—dc23
LC record available at https://lccn.loc.gov/2018021927

ISBN: 978-1-9753-5325-4

10 9 8 7 6 5 4 3 2 1

LSC-C

Printed in the United States of America

The HERO and His ELF BRIDE
Open a PIZZA PARLOR in
ANOTHER WORLD

Kaya Kizaki

ILLUSTRATION BY

Shiso

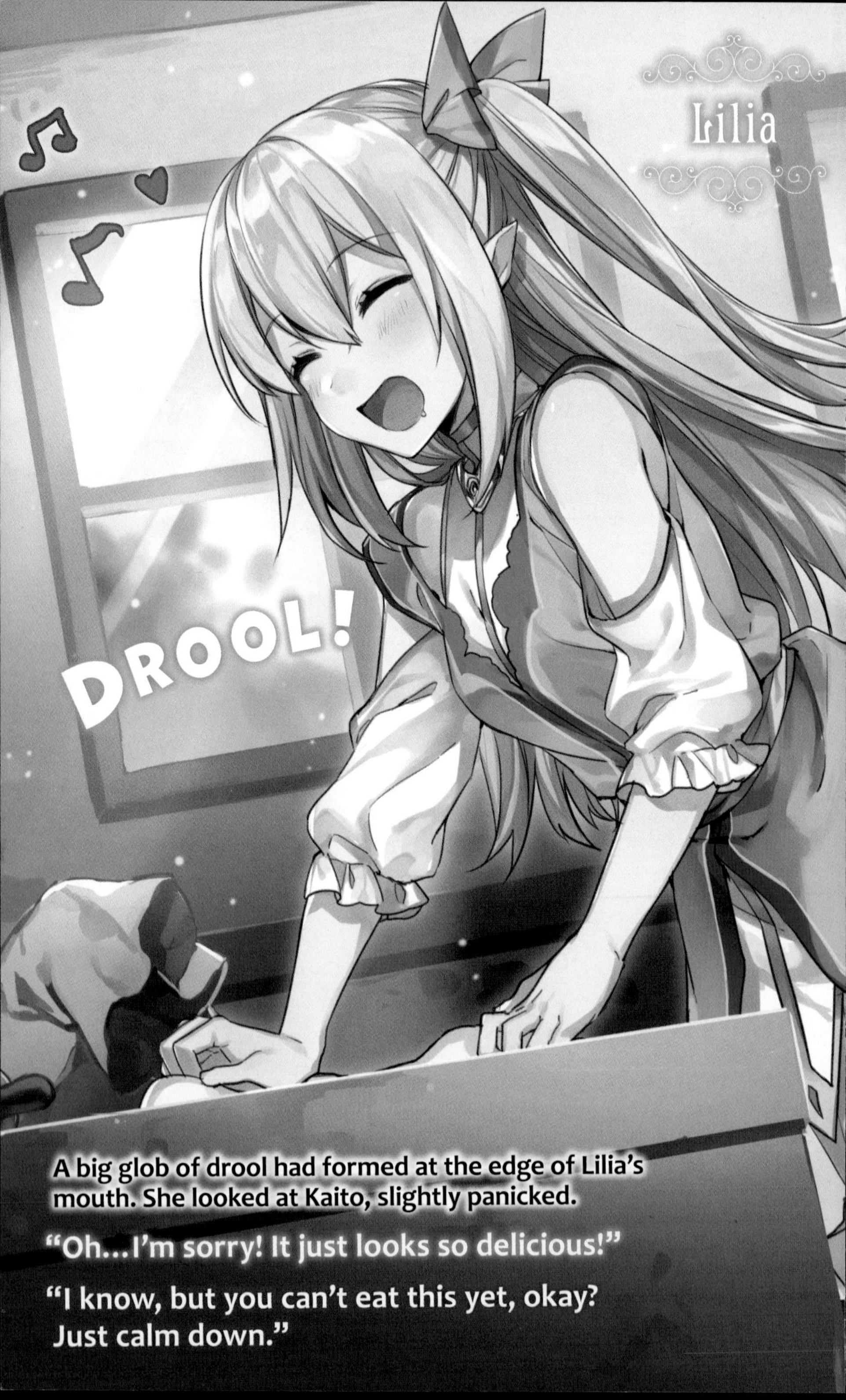
Lilia
DROOL!

A big glob of drool had formed at the edge of Lilia's mouth. She looked at Kaito, slightly panicked.

"Oh…I'm sorry! It just looks so delicious!"

"I know, but you can't eat this yet, okay? Just calm down."

Kaito

Making Pizza with
My Elf Bride

"Wait... Could that be Queen Eleonora?"

murmured Kaito.

A Delivery for the Queen

**"...Hmph, so this is pizza."**

Eleonora had her arms crossed and a suspicious look on her face, eyeing the pizza intently.

*Eleonora*

*Yow... She's gorgeous!*

No sooner had the thought crossed his mind than Kaito noticed how scant the girl's clothing was.

Almost half of her generous chest was exposed, and he was all too aware of her body heat and the softness of her skin through her thin clothing.

"Are you okay?"

"Ergh..."

Suddenly, he got the distinct feeling that someone wanted to kill him. He looked up to find Lilia staring daggers at him.

Sasha

Shopping at the Great Market

# CONTENTS

"Aw man, I'm so hungry..."

Kaito heaved a sigh of near starvation. He was so busy with work, all he'd had for breakfast was a nutrient bar.

"I can't stand it! Being hungry sucks..."

He felt like he was going to faint clean away from lack of food. He could barely think. All he could do was force himself to move his feet, one step after another, like a race walker.

"I wonder what I should eat... Ramen, curry, beef bowl, hamburger..."

He suddenly spotted a pizza delivery moped. The logo showed it was from the most popular pizza place in town.

"Ahhh, pizza... Now, that would be good... Pizza, pizza!"

It was only then that he noticed the bike wasn't slowing down.

"Pi—" was the last thing Kaito ever said.

The delivery bike slammed into him without even putting on the brakes, sending him flying through the air.

✳

When he came to, Kaito was in a beautiful castle in the sky. White clouds floated all around. There, in a chamber with a floor that shone like platinum, was a goddess.

Now, of course, Kaito had never seen a goddess, but this woman exuded such holiness that he couldn't help thinking she was one.

She wore a sparkling platinum robe and had shimmering golden hair that nearly touched the floor. She looked human at first glance, but on closer inspection, she was clearly something more.

"Um...I..."

"Welcome. Please come this way."

He approached a simple steel-frame folding chair to which she was gesturing. It didn't really look like the sort of thing that belonged in a heavenly castle.

"Sit."

"Uh, sure..."

The chair creaked as he sat down. The goddess, for her part, took a seat at a desk directly in front of him. It was a big, heavy thing that looked like it was probably made out of mahogany. Clearly classy décor. He felt like a part-timer sitting in front of the president of the company.

Facing the goddess, Kaito was struck by a wave of déjà vu. This felt an awful lot like...a job interview. It was the one strange hint of reality in an otherwise fantastical moment.

"Um..."

"Kaito, you died in a traffic accident. Do you remember?"

"Huh...?"

*Died?*

Kaito looked around again, his eyes darting back and forth. Yep: This was definitely the main hall of a bright-white sky-castle. Not the sort of place you'd expect to encounter in the normal course of your life.

"Um, is this all a...dream...?"

"No. You're dead."

*Dead... Seriously? I don't feel dead...*

The deity ignored Kaito's confusion, pulling out a bulging file folder.

"You have orders to go to another world as a hero and save that realm."

"Come again?"

"Let's get started on the paperwork."

"Hang on a second!"

*I haven't even processed being dead, but she's getting right down to business?!*

The goddess began paging through the file as if she hadn't heard him. "Excuse me… What's this about going to another world as a hero?"

*What is this, a video game?* As baffled as he was, though, he couldn't hide a hint of excitement. This was a dream. It had to be. So why not enjoy it?

"Currently, you can choose one of three different types of hero. Each comes with all the starting equipment and items required."

"Oh—oh really…"

The goddess, who up to now had spoken indifferently, stood up and announced, "Your first choice is the Holy Rose Knight, the garlanded guardian! You shall fight the monster army of an evil witch, defend the people—and the princess—of the country of the roses, and save the world!" The goddess looked down at an index card in her hand. "Your starting equipment will be the 'Holy Rose Knight Set' (Rose Sword, Rose Shield, Rose Armor, some healing potions, et cetera)."

"Ooh, a warrior type, huh? That's cool. Sword fighting is always so dramatic!"

He could just picture himself displaying his phenomenal sword work as he toppled foe after foe. Exciting!

"Your second choice is the hero of thunder, born of the storm: the Lightning Wizard! The dark mages have returned from a realm most ancient, and you must save a world threatened by evil and terrible magicks! Comes with the 'Thunder Hero Set' (Thunder Staff, robe ensemble, et cetera)."

"Getting to use magic could be fun. Rattling off complex incantations, unleashing incredible magical assaults… Sure sounds pretty good…"

He could almost see himself tossing his long robe back dramatically before summoning a massive bolt of lightning to bring down his enemies. Kaito was practically quivering with anticipation.

"Your third and final choice is the High-Calorie Hero! You shall save the all-too-herbivorous elves by bringing them delicious pizza! Starting equipment is the 'High-Calorie Set' (apron, flour, organic yeast, cheese, et cetera)."

"Huh? Save the world with pizza? 'High-Calorie' *what*? What kind of stupid hero is that?" Kaito was dumbstruck. "…I think one of these things is not like the others. Just what is a High-Calorie Hero?"

"Now then, which shall you become? Come—choose!"

"Are you ignoring me?"

"Now, then! Now, then! Now, then!"

She seemed eager to get the paperwork out of the way. She leaned forward, exhorting Kaito to make his selection. Somehow, it didn't seem so much like a dream anymore.

"Okay, I get it! All right already!"

This "High-Calorie Hero" was out of the question, so it was just a matter of whether he preferred the first choice or the second. Did he want to slice up monsters with his sword or blow them to pieces with his magic?

*Hmm, decisions, decisions... I always got stuck choosing my character class in video games. Fighters are pretty standard and pretty cool, but it's always fun wielding powerful magic.*

"Hurry up and choose. Pressure's on, kid. Come on. I wanna go home." Her tone of voice had changed as she started losing her patience. It was a little scary.

"Oh, uh, okay. Just please hold on for one second..."

Who could possibly make a snap decision when told they were going to be reincarnated as a hero? His next life hung in the balance.

*Such a pushy goddess.* He wished she'd stop drumming her fingers on the desk in annoyance. Not to mention, her pointed sighing was distracting.

At that moment, a telephone-like object on the desk rang. What was a telephone doing there?

The goddess grabbed the receiver.

"Yeah, uh-huh, that's right. This guy's still dithering. Huh? Wha—? Really? Okay, I'll tell him."

She hung up, then rose from her chair.

"While you were sitting here like an idiot, other people took choices one and two."

"Huh?"

"So by default, you get hero number three."

"Huh...?! Number three? You mean that weird pizza guy?!"

*No! No way!*

Kaito tried to protest, but a little jute bag was already being tossed at him.

"There are your items. One High-Calorie Set, as promised. You and only you can take it out of there anytime you like."

"Huh? Huh? Huh?! Wait just a darn second! You can't force me to—"

This was his second life they were talking about! There had to be more to the process than this!

But the goddess said coldly, "Go forth! Save the world! O High-Calorie Hero!!"

"That's the stupidest nickname I've ever heard!" Kaito said, but the scene in front of his eyes was already fading. Soon, he was swallowed by darkness.

# CHAPTER 2

# The High-Calorie Hero's Warm Welcome

"Aaaaaahhh!!"

Was this interdimensional travel? An instant later, Kaito found himself spit out onto an unfamiliar grass field.

"Eeyow-ow-ow! Not very gentle, are they?" Kaito grumbled. He brushed himself off and stood up.

He was surrounded by a spreading field of green. Far in the distance was an even greener forest and mountains, and over his head, white clouds drifted lazily through the bluest of skies. This was very much an idyllic, Middle Ages Europe–type fantasy world.

"O Honored Hero!!"

The shout of welcome came from behind and hit Kaito like a tidal wave, startling him. He turned nervously to find a crowd of people waving and shouting joyously. Villagers of some sort, it looked like—but then he squinted.

*Hmm? Huh? Narrow, pointy ears…? Are those…elves? Come to think of it, that goddess did say something about saving the country of the elves…*

"Ah, a pleasure to meet you."

Kaito didn't know exactly what was going on or who was speaking, but he bowed politely just the same.

"Welcome and well come, hero! I am the leader of this village, Edmond." A magisterial middle-aged man appeared and executed a formal bow. His beautiful golden hair and green eyes were the picture of elf-ness. He could've been plucked out of any number of movies or video games.

"Uh, the pleasure's all mine..."

Kaito was about to introduce himself when a naughty little thought occurred to him. What if he were to give them the name he always used in games? Or rather, the two names?

Kaito coughed and cleared his throat.

"Ahem! I am the itinerant Destiny Seeker, the Étoile Filante, Kaito!"

The name Destiny Seeker was self-explanatory. Étoile Filante was French, meaning "shooting star." It was a little over-the-top, but he liked it.

However, the names set the elves buzzing.

"Itinerant...?"

"Desh-tee-nee?"

"Ay-twal...fee...fee...?"

"What will we call him...?"

The elves' confusion was painfully clear, and Kaito blushed.

"Uh, never mind! Kaito... I'm Kaito! Just call me that!"

He felt like a politician begging for votes, but the elves seemed to understand and accept this designation.

*I can't get carried away here. God, how embarrassing.*

"In that case, Lord Kaito, please come to my home. I will be honored to accommodate you there." Kaito nodded quickly at Edmond's polite offer. He couldn't quite meet the headman's eyes, still feeling a little embarrassed.

"Y-yeah, sure."

"We shall hold a welcome feast for you tonight, so you'll meet the other villagers then."

The elves waved, sad to see him go. It was only then that he realized how focused they were on him.

Elves, of course, were usually depicted as being quite smart and trim, but these people had gone beyond thin into what looked like starvation territory. He was a little surprised they could hold themselves up while they walked.

Come to think of it, hadn't he been told his mission was to help them with "high calories"?

*That goddess was in such a hurry to get me out of there; I wish she'd taken the time to explain things a little more clearly...*

"Now please come this way."

They walked along a road flanked by fields, at the end of which was the headman's mansion. It was a big two-story building, but it could hardly be called luxurious. Like the elves themselves, it seemed somehow wasted away.

"Beside the mansion is the shop you shall run, Honored Hero."

There was a little store for Kaito's benefit next to the big house. He peeked inside and found a stone oven and a countertop—it was a pizza kitchen. The setup was simple, but it was obvious they'd put their whole hearts into readying it for him.

"The goddess told us a hero would be coming to our aid, so we made sure to have this prepared. The oven has been heating for several days, so you should be able to use it immediately. Ah, you have no idea with what anticipation we've been awaiting you!"

"......"

Kaito didn't say anything. It sounded like they'd been waiting a pretty long time. It probably just went to show that nobody wanted to pick the "High-Calorie Hero." Kaito had a feeling this role had been foisted on him, but it was a little late to be worried about that.

"Thank you very much," he said. "I appreciate your taking care of things."

For the time being, there was nothing to do but give it a shot.

✳

He settled into his room, and before he knew it, it was evening.

There was a hesitant knock at the door, accompanied by a girl's voice.

"Lord Kaito, may I come in?"

"Oh, sure."

"Thank you." She entered the room carefully—an elf girl with long, strawberry-blond hair and green eyes. She was probably about high school age. If they had "high school" in this world, that was.

The strawberry-blond elf wouldn't quite look at him, as if she was feeling shy.

"Pleased to meet you. My name is Lilia. My father asked me to come look after you."

"Your father...?"

"The headman, Edmond."

"Ahhh, so you're his daughter."

Lilia gave a small nod. When Kaito turned to her, she blushed and turned her eyes to the floor. She was the retiring type, apparently.

"If I may, shall I show you to the banquet?"

"Thanks. I just got here, and I don't know my right hand from my left. I appreciate the help!"

As he followed Lilia down the stairs, the buzz of conversation reached his ears. Lilia pushed open two large double doors, and he saw bright lights and began to make out distinct voices. It was a massive chamber, and all the villagers were already waiting for him. When they saw Kaito, they started to applaud.

"Honored Hero!"

"Lord Kaito!"

He saw a banner with HERO'S WELCOME PARTY written across it fluttering gently.

Kaito, who had never been the subject of so much attention in his life, stepped sheepishly into the room. About the only time he had ever been the guest of honor at a party was, maybe, his birthday in elementary school. And even back then, he'd been oddly embarrassed by it.

A group of young elf women were whispering among themselves by the wall.

"So that's him..."

"Incredible! Look at that black hair..."

When he glanced in their direction, they shrieked and ran away laughing.

He could definitely see how he might look unusual to the elves.

"This seat is for you, Lord Kaito," Lilia said.

It looked like they had forgone tables and chairs, perhaps because of the number of people present. Instead, there were cushions set out on a carpet. Kaito sat down. He felt like he had walked into the *Arabian Nights*.

"Here, have some wine." A silver cup was being filled with a purplish-red liquid. *Wine, huh? Smells good.*

Then he noticed Edmond sidling up next to him.

"Thank you all for coming to this, the welcome feast for our hero, Lord Kaito!" the village leader declared. "As headman, I thank you! I have brought out food and drink specially from our stores, and tonight, I urge you to enjoy yourselves to your hearts' content!"

The silver cup was extended to Kaito.

"Here's to the advent of a hero in our benighted world! Cheers!"

"Cheers!"

"Oh... Thanks. Uh, cheers..."

Words like *welcome* and *advent* made him uncomfortable. He still didn't feel like much of a hero, high-calorie or otherwise.

As Kaito sipped at his drink, he suddenly found a plate being thrust at him. It was piled with a mountain of green vegetables. A salad of some kind, maybe.

"Please eat up!" Lilia was giving him an innocent smile. Kaito felt his heart rate spike.

"S-sure...!" He reflexively looked away from her. *This is dangerous... That girl is way too cute.*

"It's delicious."

*Nom, nom, nom, nom, nom.* Lilia dug into the vegetables on the plate.

"W-wait, didn't you bring that for me?"

"Of course. Please have some."

"Have some? There's nothing left but leaves!" Kaito stabbed desperately at a lingering bit of green with his fork.

*Th-this is a competition...!*

"Hmm...?" He frowned as he chewed on the leaflike vegetable.

*What the heck? This is awful! There's no taste at all! Couldn't they at least put some salt on it?*

*It feels like I'm just eating a mouthful of grass from a random field around here. What am I, a horse?*

"What do you think? They're freshly picked." Lilia was still beaming.

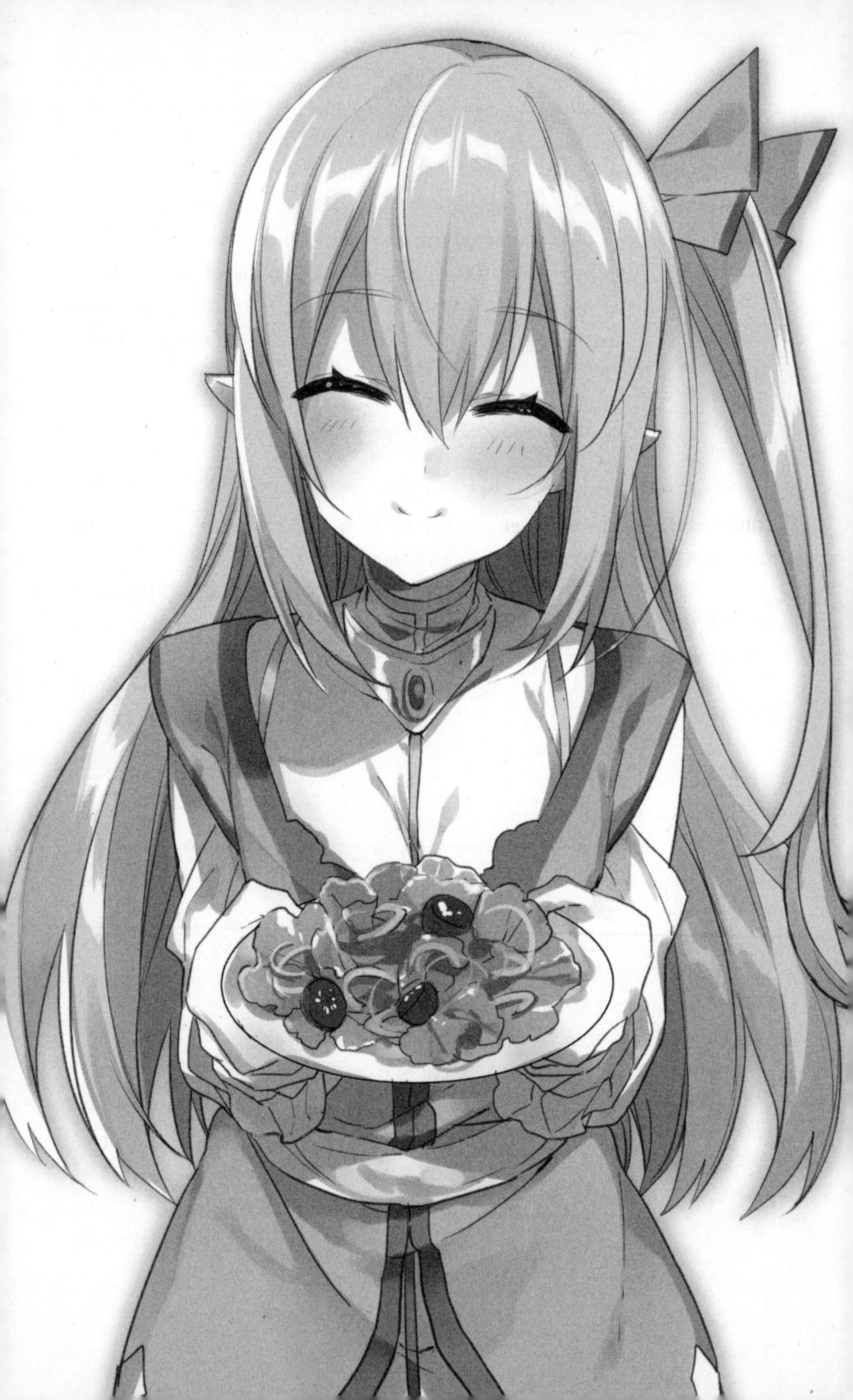

He somehow managed to smile back at her. It would be rude to tell her he thought it was terrible.

"Try some of this, too."

There were more vegetables on the next plate offered. He stole a glance at the banquet table and found leafy greens staring back at him from all the other dishes as well. Apparently, this was what passed for a feast in this world. It was all vegetables! How would he ever feel full? No wonder the elves all looked so emaciated.

*I need something richer! Something robust and filling!*

"......"

He was grateful for the welcome feast, but not so much for the welcome food. It was almost entirely vegetables, and the ham-like meat he finally managed to find had a weak and unsatisfying flavor.

"Now that this banquet is well and truly underway," Edmond announced, "it's time for a word from our hero."

Kaito nodded to Edmond and boldly got to his feet. He had obtained the power of pizza, and his heart burned with furious passion. He would teach these people what delicious food truly was!

"Thank you very much, everyone, for doing all this for me! To show my gratitude, I'm going to make something delicious for you tomorrow!"

There was a happy shout from the assembled crowd and a round of applause.

He would bring them THE POWER OF PIZZA!

*...Dang. That doesn't sound cool at all.*

# CHAPTER 3

# Kaito Makes His First Pizza

Kaito awoke in a room on the second floor of the headman's mansion.

"Ugh... I'm sooo hungry..."

Ninety percent of what he'd eaten at the feast the night before had been vegetables. He hardly felt full at all.

There was a knock at the door, and Lilia came in. "Good morning, Lord Kaito," she said. "Breakfast is ready."

"Oh, uh, th-thanks..."

He sat up groggily. Whatever they'd put out for breakfast, he was sure it would be the same unsatisfying fare as the night before. With his stomach growling pitifully, Kaito got out of bed.

"Eek!" Lilia gave a little shriek and put her hands to her face.

"Huh?" Kaito grunted, looking down at himself. His pajama shirt was rumpled and rolled up, exposing his belly button. "Oh! Sorry." He quickly smoothed the shirt out, covering himself.

"N-no, it's all right..." Lilia had turned red up to her pointy ears, fidgeting from the shock. It was really very cute.

"I'm gonna get changed, and then I'll come eat," Kaito said.

"Right!" Lilia all but bolted out of the room, and Kaito began putting on his clothes.

✳

Breakfast at the headman's house consisted of piles of vegetables, a dry, flavorless bread, and fried eggs. Nothing had much taste. Umami was conspicuously lacking around here.

Since they were offering him their hospitality, Kaito naturally felt he couldn't complain, but neither could he muster much enthusiasm.

"Thank you for the meal. Now let's get ready for a feast!"

"I eagerly await!"

When he saw the anticipation in Edmond's eyes, Kaito felt a twinge of anxiety.

*Do I even really know how to make a pizza? They can call me the High-Calorie Hero all they want, but I don't know anything about pizza. And I've certainly never made one.*

Deeply concerned, Kaito headed for the little shop beside the mansion. He stood at the counter by the oven and let out a sigh. "Okay then, where to start? We don't even have ingredients..."

The only thing he had with him was the item pouch the goddess had given him when she sent him here. He rifled through it and found it had several cards inside.

"Hmm. Let's see here..."

He examined the cards he'd pulled out. Each bore the name of something that sounded like it would be useful in the kitchen, like *Black Apron*, *Pizza Skill 1*, and *Wheat Flour*.

"What do I do with these?" *That goddess should've done her job properly. I don't even know how to use any of my starter items!* Kaito inspected the cards closely. "Do I have to exchange them somewhere? I don't think I've seen any place like that..."

For a long moment, he stared at one. "Uhhh, *'Black Apron'*?" He tried saying it aloud.

No sooner had he done so than the card disappeared from his hand, and he found himself holding a black apron instead.

"Ohhh! So I just read the names out loud!"

It was pretty simple once you knew how it worked. The goddess had told Kaito that only he could use these items. In other words, if someone else got their hands on them, they'd just be regular cards. Kaito alone could turn them into useful tools.

"I get it now. That's pretty clever." Putting the items in card form made them easy to carry—very convenient for interdimensional travel.

Kaito started by tying the strings of the black apron around his waist.

"So this is a hero's equipment, huh?" he said with a wry smile. He had to admit it wasn't bad. He thought he could feel himself standing a little straighter. "Okay, ingredients. *Water, Wheat Flour, Yeast, Salt.*" One by one, the items appeared on the countertop as Kaito read them out.

"Wait, what's this? *'Peel'*?"

When he recited the unfamiliar word, something like a long-handled spatula appeared in front of him. There were two of them, one with a wooden blade and one with metal. "Oh, so this is that thing you use to put the pizza in the oven..."

Finally, he held the last card in his hand. On it was written *Pizza Skill 1 (Pizza Basics).* The fact that this card said "1" suggested there was a "2." He turned the card over and found something written in small letters on the back:

*To achieve Pizza Skill 2, make a margherita!*

*Margherita* he understood. It was a simple but delicious pie featuring mozzarella cheese and basil over tomato sauce.

*I see. I need to complete missions to gain new skill cards. So that's how this works. Maybe I'll get additional ingredients and tools as I need them, too.*

"Pizza Skill 1!" Kaito exclaimed, and suddenly, he found his brain full of the knowledge of how to prepare and bake a pizza. His understanding had increased instantaneously.

"Awesome!!"

At that moment, there was a halting knock at the door.

"Yes, come in."

"I'll assist you..."

Someone entered in a trembling wave of anxiety. It was the headman's only daughter, Lilia. She kept her eyes on the floor, but despite her display of reluctance, she came right up to him.

*What's the deal here? Is she into me...? I mean, she's cute, but she's just gonna get in the way.*

"It's fine. I can handle it myself."

"Oh..."

Lilia recoiled from him as if she'd been slapped, and her green eyes went wide. "B-but it's a wife's duty..."

"Huh? Wife?" He looked at her, uncomprehending. "Who's whose wife here?"

"Lord Kaito, I'm your..."

Kaito balked at this sudden claim. He had just been about to start making a pizza, and now some sort of marriage decree had thrown a wrench in those plans, smashing them to pieces.

"No, no, no, wait, wait, *wife*? What do you mean?"

"My father instructed me to look after everything for you, Lord Kaito."

"Hmm? That doesn't necessarily make you my wife, does it?"

"Well, I—"

Lilia blushed fiercely. "I'm just about the right age to get married, and anyway, it's... It's what I want, too."

Her voice grew quieter and quieter as she spoke, until Kaito had to lean in to hear her. "Huh? What was that last part?"

"Uh-uh! I can't say it again!!"

"OW!!"

Lilia gave him a hearty smack on the shoulder, making him cry out.

*Yikes, that stings. This girl's stronger than she looks. Maybe she really could help me with the pizza. It takes a fair amount of stamina, after all.* Maybe it was his new status as the High-Calorie Hero that seemingly had all his thoughts revolving around pizza.

"D-do you hate me that much...?" Lilia's huge green eyes began to swim, and then comically large tears started rolling down her cheeks. Her long ears drooped pitifully.

"H-hang on, now...!" Kaito hadn't made a girl cry since elementary school. With no idea what to do, he grew mildly panicked.

"I guess I'm just not the right girl for you," Lilia said. She covered her face with her hands, her shoulders heaving.

"N-no! That's not it..."

"I promise I'll do my best, so...so please... *Hic!*"

"Look, I just—"

"I'm still immature, but I'm sure I'll— *Sniff! Hic!*"

"Aaaaarrrgh!"

Though weeping like a little girl, she showed no sign of backing down. Kaito found himself cornered.

"O-okay. Come on. Let's just… Let's just make a pizza for now, okay?"

Lilia's face was instantly shining again. "Yes, sir! I'd be thrilled to!"

"……"

*Hang on a second. I didn't say I'd marry her or anything, right? What's with the giant smile?*

But he could hardly say any of this to the glowing Lilia. Kaito had the sneaking suspicion he was now engaged, but he decided not to dwell on it.

*One thing's for sure—I'm hungry as hell. I wanna get that pizza made, then stuff it in my mouth.*

"All right, pizza time."

"Yes, sir!"

"Just so you know, the food we know as pizza originated in the port city of Naples, in a country called Italy. It began as a bread-like foodstuff enjoyed by the fishermen there, and when tomatoes were introduced from South America, it took on the form we know today."

*Holy crap. Where'd all this trivia come from? My mouth is moving on its own.*

"Emigrants from the south of Italy brought pizza to America at the end of the nineteenth century, and it arrived in my country, Japan, in 1956. In other words, it's a relatively new food for the Japanese."

Lilia's eyes were closed, her head bobbing rhythmically up and down. *She's not even listening!! In fact, she's asleep!*

"Ahem! Shall we get started, then?"

Lilia's eyes popped open. *Is the history of pizza that boring…?*

Kaito tried to collect himself. "So, first, we're going to put all the ingredients in a big bowl."

The steps of the recipe came readily to his mind. First, you put water in a bowl and add salt. It's important to make sure the salt is completely dissolved in the water.

"Next, we take the wheat flour and… Hey, what are you doing?!"

Lilia had buried her face in the bag of flour.

"I thought it might smell nice. Flour is very rare. I don't see it often."

"Uh, sure. But let's not stick our faces in the ingredients, okay? Could you put in half the bag of flour?"

Lilia was turning out to be a somewhat stranger girl than he'd thought, but she poured the wheat flour into the bowl.

*Now work it with your hands to mix it in. When it gets thick, add the yeast.*

"Ooh, it's got a little stick to it now," observed Kaito. It was starting to look like he'd have enough dough to feed a whole crowd. It took a fair amount of strength to work it. "Now put in half of what's left of the flour."

Lilia obediently added the ingredients. *I've got to admit, it's nice having a helper.*

"You're so good at this, Lord Kaito! It's amazing how you know exactly what to do!"

"Ha-ha, well...that's 'cause I'm a hero!"

*The way she looks at me reverently like that... I could get used to this.*

*If I'm gonna be a hero, I might as well practice looking good!*

Kaito had always thought of men who could cook as if they came from some other dimension, but now that he was among their number, he found he was enjoying himself.

*The High-Calorie Hero... Yeah, that's not so bad. Even if it's not the greatest nickname in the world.*

Kaito grabbed the dough, vigorously forming it into a ball. His body was moving on its own now. He would never have been able to work this smoothly before. Apparently, being a real-life hero had its perks, even if his powers were a bit unconventional.

The dough had started to toughen, so he began mixing in the remaining flour, turning the dough periodically. When the dough was one big ball, he started kneading it again. It took more than a little strength; the sweat starting to bead on his forehead was proof.

"Knead! Knead! Kneadkneadkneadknead!!"

He suddenly got more and more enthusiastic, until he realized he was actually shouting.

"Lord Kaito, you're amazing! Look how much dough we have already!" Lilia applauded him, but Kaito, embarrassed, could only nod. Was it the skill card that had made him so passionate about pizza?

"Phew...". The sweat was on his temples now. He was grateful when Lilia gently wiped it away with a cloth.

*I've got the ability now, but my stamina just isn't what it used to be. This is tough work. Bet my muscles are gonna hurt tomorrow...*

"Shall we trade places?" Lilia asked.

"Huh? This is pretty tough, you know." Even though he was a fit young man, Kaito could already feel his arms going limp as noodles.

"But you seem to be struggling, and I've watched you long enough to know how to do the work."

"Oh yeah? Give it a try, then."

He wanted to cook the pizza that night, so there was no time to rest. Kaito decided to let Lilia take over the kneading.

"Hup! And hup!" As Kaito looked on anxiously, Lilia began working the dough.

"Erm, so, uh, try to grab it, put a little strength into it—"

"Like this?"

"No, not quite. More like this." Kaito placed his hands over Lilia's.

"Oh!!" She pulled her hands back, surprised. Her pointy ears quivered.

"Huh? Oh, sorry."

"No, I was just...a little shocked..."

Lilia's face was bright red. *Guess I got so caught up in the work that I wasn't sensitive enough toward her.*

"Want to keep trying? I'll just watch."

"Okay." Lilia began assiduously working the dough. She didn't quite have the knack yet, but she was definitely going in the right direction.

"Knead! Knead! Kneadkneadkneadkneadknead!!"

Suddenly, Lilia started shouting, and Kaito was stunned. "E-everything all right?"

She stared back at him, equally mystified. "I'm just doing it like you did, Lord Kaito..."

"No, no yelling! You don't need to yell! You just need to knead!"

"Oh, I see," Lilia said, looking a little disappointed.

*You know, I keep wondering if this girl is quite...all there...*

"Okay, now we're gonna add the last of the flour bit by bit."

But at that moment, Lilia stopped moving.

"Are you okay? Are you tired?"

*Drooool...* A big glob of drool had formed at the edge of Lilia's mouth.

She looked at Kaito, slightly panicked. "Oh...I'm sorry! It just looks so delicious!"

"I know, but you can't eat this yet, okay? Just calm down."

"Yes, sir..."

Kaito, now anxious for a different reason, watched Lilia work again. He was very concerned she would drool in the dough—or perhaps start eating it.

"Just let me know if you get tired, and we can switch back."

"Okay!"

But in the end, Lilia finished all the kneading. Maybe elves had more strength than their thin bodies let on.

When they took a good look at the dough after thirty minutes of kneading, they found the surface smooth and shiny, and it no longer stuck to the bowl. When they tugged at the dough, it stretched into a thin layer.

"Perfect. This is great." Kaito picked up the dough and put it on the countertop. Then he started pressing it from left to right, then right to left. Then from the center outward. With each movement, he tapped the dough gently, working the material into the perfect shape.

"Wow... That looks really difficult, but you do it so smoothly! Amazing!"

"Thanks." It was true—this would be tricky for a beginner, but thanks to Kaito's skill card, he managed it easily.

"Why do you push on the dough like that?"

"It helps build up layers of gas inside." The words were rolling off his tongue now, but the explanation seemed lost on Lilia, who half nodded.

Kaito repeated this process about a dozen times until the dough was a nice, round ball. Then he scored a cross-shaped mark into the top with a knife. Several gas bubbles popped up from the incision.

"Now, that's good dough!" Kaito wrapped the whole thing in a damp cloth. "Next, we're going to let it ferment, so it's gotta sit for a few hours."

"Sure thing! I can't wait!"

The work was hard, but Kaito felt surprisingly invigorated. Looking at the beautiful dough gave him a deep sense of satisfaction.

*It turns out it's fun to work with your hands!*

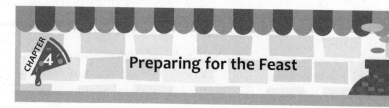

"Okay, while we wait for the dough to ferment, we're going to get the oven ready. We want it to heat slowly over a few hours until it's nice and hot." The knowledge came readily to Kaito's mind. It took time not only to make the dough but also to heat the oven. Making a pizza was harder work than he'd thought.

"I've never seen such a big oven before..." Lilia peered into the domed oven in deep interest. "What do we do first?"

"We need some small- and medium-sized firewood, stuff that will light easily." Kaito picked up some of the firewood that had been prepared for him. He put five sticks of the right size into the oven; then he lit a piece of paper on fire and put it in as well. Then he added more wood. It was important to gradually progress to bigger and bigger pieces.

"Wow! It's really burning now, isn't it?"

"Yeah, this looks good."

The two of them looked into the oven and then at each other. Kaito found Lilia was much closer to him than he'd realized, and he scrambled back.

*Oh man! Our noses were practically touching!* Lilia turned red and looked at the floor.

"Now all we have to do is wait."

No sooner had Kaito spoken than a knock came at the door.

"Lord Kaito, I've brought lunch." In came Fiona, the headman's wife.

She was also Lilia's mother, and the family resemblance was obvious. Fiona looked young enough to be Lilia's older sister. She had her long strawberry-blond hair tied in back. There was a certain calmness to her.

"It's not much, but..."

She unwrapped the parcel she had brought to reveal sandwiches. They consisted of a heap of vegetables between two pieces of bread. Kaito would have given anything for a pork cutlet sandwich, but he would just have to keep quiet for now.

"Thank you very much."

"If I may ask, is—is Lilia being helpful?" Fiona appeared a bit concerned.

"Yes, very!" She inspired a little anxiety in him from time to time, but she had certainly done her part in making the dough.

Fiona smiled happily at his response. "I'm so glad to hear it. I've tried to make sure she knows how to cook and sew. Truth be told, she's not much of a seamstress, so she's still taking lessons..."

"......"

*Am I imagining things, or does it sound like she's trying to sell me on a future wife?*

He recalled his earlier discussion with Lilia about marriage. They had kept things vague, but who knew what that meant? However, he also got the feeling any excessive questions would come back to bite him.

"I know that, as her mother, I might be biased, but I think she'll make an excellent wife for you, Hero."

"Ah...er..." As he had stood ruminating, Fiona beat him to the punch.

"Please take good care of my precious daughter." She bowed her head deeply and then quickly left the store.

"Um...?"

*Goddesses, elf-mothers... Why won't anyone around here listen to what I'm actually saying?!*

Kaito had reached out as if to stop Fiona from going, but now he let his arm fall limply back by his side. Lilia was beaming at him with a bright smile.

*Ergh... I can't shake the sense that I'm being forced into a corner here. But I've got to deal with my stomach first. All this hard work has me at max hunger!*

"Bon appétit!" Kaito and Lilia dug into their sandwiches.

"......"

*Vegetables... Tasteless, just tasteless. It's like I'm eating grass here! Frankly, it's totally unappetizing!*

Kaito worked his way through his meal uninterestedly. *I'm not getting any energy from this at all. I know I was never the most conscientious eater, but at least it fueled me up.*

It made him appreciate afresh the importance of good food.

"Hey, do you guys always eat food this bori... I mean, do you always eat vegetarian?"

"That's right. It's the way our queen does things. She believes eating plenty of vegetables leads to a beautiful body."

"Huh... So you go out of your way to eat leafy greens?" He would never have figured it was national policy. "Not a lot of meat and fish, right?"

"Mainly vegetables and fruits. We have to import most of our meat, fish, and wheat, so they're expensive..."

"I see..." The plain food definitely didn't give the impression that this was a prosperous place. Plates full of plant life might sound idyllic and in tune with nature, but really it looked like this nation just couldn't afford anything better.

"Our country is inland, surrounded by mountains and forests, so it's not easy to transport goods here."

"Yeah, I can see where that wouldn't be very convenient..."

Kaito reflected that it would be nice if he could help improve the trade situation at some point, and the elves' unbalanced diet bothered him. Even though he'd only just arrived, Kaito found himself deeply concerned for his new home.

※

About two hours later, after he had checked the state of the dough's fermentation, Kaito looked in the oven. The bricks inside the dome-shaped construction glowed white.

"Yeah, it's at a good temperature now." Kaito used the steel-bladed peel to clean out the interior, then wiped the utensil with a damp rag. "Okay! Our oven is good to go!"

"So we can bake a pizza now?" Lilia looked at him excitedly.

"Yep. We can cook it up anytime we like. All that's left is to shape the dough, put on the toppings, and—"

He stopped in midsentence when he realized they didn't have any ingredients. He had planned on making a simple margherita pizza, but that required tomato sauce, mozzarella cheese, basil leaves, and olive oil.

"I-ingredients!! Toppings!!"

"Is everything all right?" Lilia seemed concerned for the panicked Kaito.

"Lilia, do you know what mozzarella cheese is?"

"Cheese I understand, but it's something we have to import, so it's very expensive."

"......"

Kaito stood dumbstruck as it sank in that he was completely broke. Not so much as a penny...

*I thought some cash was supposed to be a standard starting item! That stupid, stupid goddess...!! Maybe she forgot to give it to me?*

He knew he was grasping at straws, but he reached into his item pouch anyway.

"Huh?" There was a rustling sound. He realized there were more cards in the pouch than there had been before. "Whoa, whoa, whoa!!" He pulled them out and found they bore the names of precisely the ingredients he needed at that moment. "Oh, thank god!!"

So apparently, the system was that he got more cards as he needed them. Since the oven was ready and the dough was done fermenting, he'd been given the tools for the next step.

He put a hand to his chest, deeply relieved.

✳

Kaito watched the clock, letting the dough ferment until evening. It would be time for the feast soon. He'd better get started. The pizza would only bake for around ninety seconds, but they had to form the dough and add the toppings first.

"*Mozzarella Cheese*!! *Tomatoes*!!" he read aloud from the cards.

"Eeeeeeek!!"

Kaito stopped, surprised, when Lilia screamed. "What is it? What's wrong?"

"That's amazing!! The cards turn into ingredients!!"

That made sense. He couldn't blame anyone for being surprised upon seeing it happen for the first time.

"What's going on? Is this magic? Can you use magic, too, Lord Kaito?"

"Er, um, well, kinda..."

It would be a pain to explain it, so he just sort of trailed off. Frankly, he didn't even really understand how it worked himself. He would have to bug the goddess about it next time he saw her.

Lilia gave a sigh of admiration. "That's really incredible... Surely, only the most accomplished magic user could do such a thing. And only after many years of study at an advanced magical university..."

"Wow, really?"

"You have to have exceptional intelligence to be able to use magic. People who can do it usually end up serving at the palace."

"Whoa..."

Of course an elf world would have magic.

Lilia picked up the bag of mozzarella cheese. "What's this?"

"It's mozzarella cheese. Wanna try a bite?"

"May I?!" She took a handful of the shredded cheese and stuffed it in her mouth. Her face went red. "What a rich flavor!! I've never tasted anything so delicious before!!"

"I'm glad you like it."

"It's truly incredible!" Lilia grabbed more of the cheese, putting it in her mouth so fast her hand became a blur.

*Munch, munch, munch, munch.*

"U-um, that's enough, now! We need that! I said a *bite*!!"

Lilia was already up to about twenty.

"Oh, I'm sorry... It just made me feel so energized!"

*Nom, nom, nom, nom, nom, nom, nom.*

Smiling broadly, Lilia continued shoving cheese into her face. Her hand dipped in and out of the bag, showing no sign of slowing down.

"No, you've got to stop! We'll run out of cheese!"

"Oh! I'm so sorry!" When Lilia finally regained control of herself, about a third of the cheese was gone. "I-I'm very sorry..." She looked down dejectedly.

"......"

For a while now, Kaito had been unable to shake the feeling that Lilia reminded him of something, and now he knew what. She was just like a pet dog he used to have: plenty of appetite and suitably ashamed when scolded for getting into food it shouldn't have.

"Wait till later! When the pizza's done cooking, you can have as much as you like, okay?"

"Okay..." Lilia sounded repentant, but he couldn't help noticing how her eyes kept flitting back to the ingredients.

*She has a serious appetite for someone so small...*

He took half the cheese and put it in a bowl with a strainer inside. He intended to wash it but couldn't concentrate for fear of what Lilia might be doing.

"Say, Lilia..."

"Yes!" Lilia looked at him, her beautiful, emerald-like eyes shining.

"I've got a job for you."

"Anything!"

"To enjoy making pizza, you need a rhythm. Slap the countertop with the peels—gently, okay? Hold one in each hand." He passed her the wooden and metal peels.

"Okay!" Lilia began smacking them to a beat.

*Good, both her hands are full! Now I can concentrate!*

He opened the canned tomatoes and put them in the bowl. The bright-red color made them look delicious.

"Hey, what's that?"

"I'm making tomato sauce."

"...It looks great." *Drool.*

"Calm down, Lilia! Keep your hands moving!"

"Right!" She hurriedly went back to clapping the peels against the counter.

Kaito added a bit of salt and began mashing the tomatoes with his fingers. "It's important not to smoosh the tomatoes so much that they get completely smooth. Leaving them a little chunky adds to the tactile experience."

*Drool.*

".......... "

It was like having a monster with an empty stomach right next to him. Kaito nervously continued working on the pizza.

"Okay, time to shape the dough." Kaito dusted the dough with flour, getting rid of the excess white powder. This was where he would really get to show off his skills. That might sound strange coming from someone who had never made a pizza before, but thanks to the skill card, he was as confident as a lifelong chef.

"You use four fingers on each hand, excluding your thumb, to stretch the dough. Use the pads of your fingers." He pulled the dough from the center out toward the edge. It was tricky ensuring it was stretched evenly, but with Kaito's newfound abilities, he didn't have any problems. "You want to leave about a centimeter along the edge untouched. That allows the gases in the dough to move to the end." He flipped it around, changed the angle slightly, and continued stretching it. He progressed steadily, stretch, stretch, stretch. "Make it round, make it round, nice and even."

"Make it round, make it round, nice and even."

Lilia mimicked Kaito's tone. Suddenly realizing he was practically humming, he quickly closed his mouth.

He started by making four round discs of dough.

"Done! Now for the toppings." He put plenty of tomato sauce in the center of each disc, running a spoon along it in a spiral to spread it. The trick was to deliberately introduce some inconsistencies so it wasn't too smooth. And of course, he left one centimeter from the edge bare.

Next, he took the mozzarella cheese, sliced it into two- or three-millimeter pieces, and added it to the pizzas, taking care that it didn't clump anywhere.

"And now the basil... Oh." He didn't have a basil card. "That's no good. Lilia, do you know what basil is?"

"No, sir!"

"Didn't think so. Do you have any leafy herbs?"

"The garden is full of edible plants..."

Kaito had her escort him there immediately.

"Hmm..." Kaito glanced around the garden. "This! This looks just like basil!" He chose one of the flavorless leaves he'd been served at the feast the night before. Kaito had never had any sort of green thumb in the past, but thanks to his skill card, he now knew just which plant he needed.

"Oh, that's parjee. It has a wonderful smell."

"Parjee...!!" Kaito gently picked a leaf and held it to his nose. "You're right—it smells fantastic!! It's a lot like basil!" He immediately pulled off several parjee leaves and put them on the pizzas. Not only did they smell wonderful, but they added a rich green color to the food.

"Aroma and freshness are the most important things, so we leave these for last." Finally, he added a dash of olive oil in a spiral pattern, and the pizzas were ready.

"They look SOOOO GOOOOD...!" Excited, Lilia leaned in to take a close look at the food. Kaito, sensing danger, quickly moved them away from her.

"Now all we have to do is bake them. Calm down, Lilia! Give me one of the peels."

She passed him the wood-bladed one, and he dusted it with flour. He put the pizza on the peel and added some finishing touches to the shape. Then, he ever so carefully put the concoction in the oven. He would be baking four pizzas at once, so he started with the spot farthest from the fire and worked his way over.

This being his first attempt, he was a little nervous, but he knew all the right steps. After about thirty seconds, the dough started rising, so he lifted the edge with a peel specifically for turning pizzas and made sure everything was getting enough heat.

"All right!"

It was browning up nicely, so he turned it 180 degrees so the other side could cook, too. He did the same for the other three pizzas. All of them were coming out just right. It was surprisingly physical labor, and looking into the oven made him hot. The sight of the well-cooked pizzas was exciting, though. A delicious scent tickled his nose, and he could hear his own stomach rumbling.

"They're done!" Kaito pulled the freshly baked pies out of the oven and set them on the countertop. They were burned here and there, just like they should be, and the crust had puffed up perfectly. The cheese was thick and melted, while the parjee had settled nicely into the tomato sauce. The delightful contrast between red and white and green definitely sharpened the appetite. Just looking at it was enough to make his mouth water. Yes: These pizzas looked very, very good.

Kaito sliced them with a pizza cutter.

"Lilia, give it a taste test."

"...May I?" She looked at him doubtfully, like a dog that had been told to sit and stay for too long.

"Sure! You helped make it; you ought to get the first bite."

"Thank you!"

Lilia gently picked up a slice.

"Ow, ow, ow, ow!!"

"Careful. It's hot."

Lilia blew on the pizza to cool it down. Despite being sensitive to the heat, she brought the slice to her mouth.

*The moment of truth. Will my pizza really be suited to the elves' taste?* Kaito watched Lilia's reaction with no small amount of trepidation.

"Wooooooow! It's so soft and chewy and rich and gooey!!"

Kaito jumped at Lilia's ecstatic exclamation. Her face melted much the way the cheese had. *"Fwaaa...* It's sooo...delicious..."

He knew she was telling the truth when the slice disappeared only seconds later.

"Thanks! But there's some cheese hanging from your mouth..."

"Amazing... I've never eaten anything so delicious in my entire life. It smells wonderful, and it's thick and juicy and satisfying..."

Lilia was completely enraptured.

Kaito was relieved and excited at the same time.

*Excellent! I'm gonna have them eat even more delicious food!*

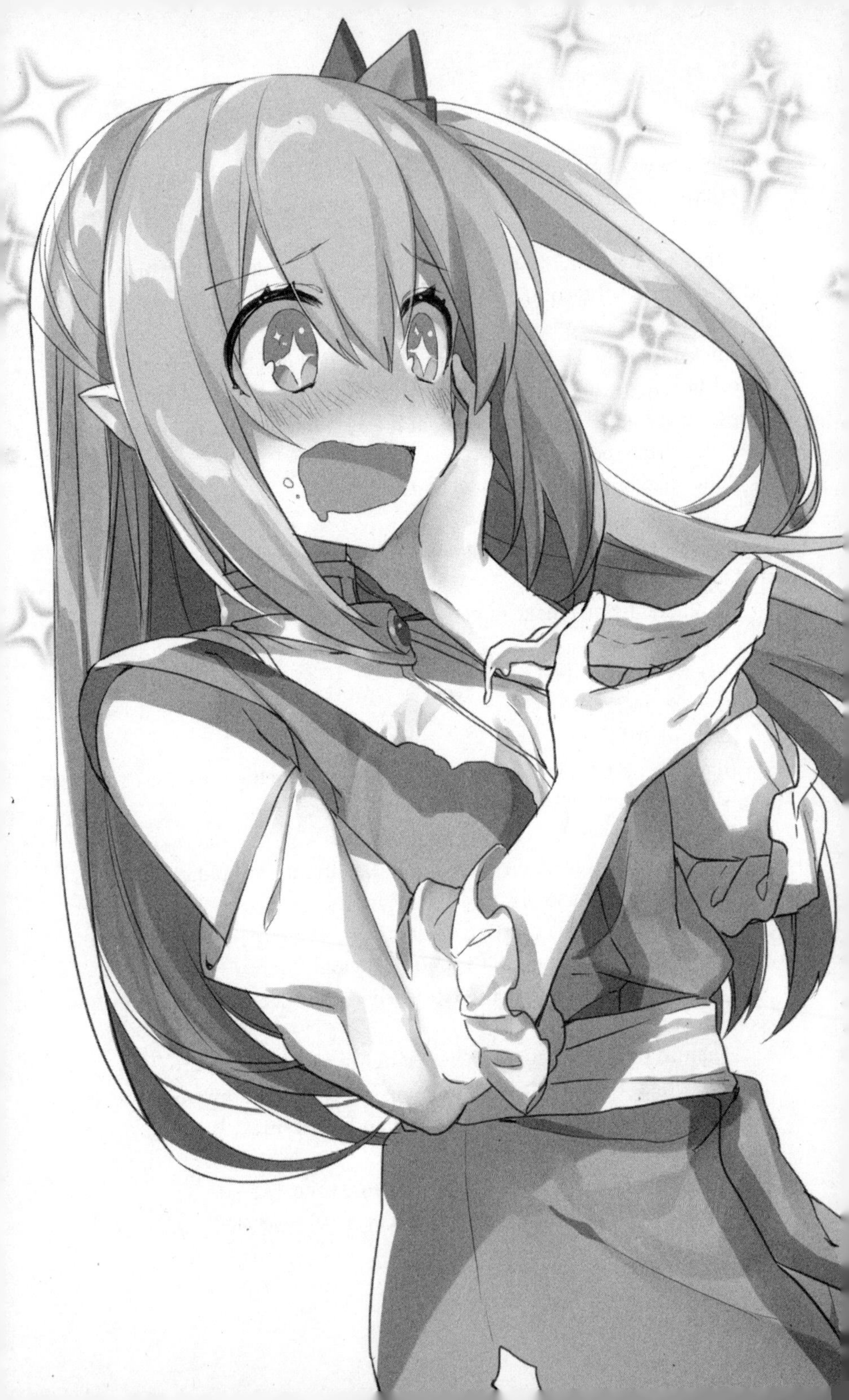

"Okay, let's get baking! Bring 'em on over!"

"Yes, sir!!"

∗

When Kaito had finished baking all the pizzas, he took one plate for himself and then headed for the feast. When he appeared, a murmur spread among the gathered villagers.

"All right, everyone, let's eat!! Here it is, the hero's pizza!!"

The villagers made a beeline for the long-awaited treat. There was a moment's silence, and then a great shout went up:

"Whoooooooooooaaaaaaa!!"

"It's delicious!!"

"What is this? What *is* this??"

The elves' faces lit up in ecstasy, and they turned their passionate eyes on Kaito.

"This is the first time I've ever had anything so wonderful!"

"What richness! I can practically feel it strengthening me!"

"The flavor spreads through your mouth... It just keeps going and going!!"

The elves were all but shaking with emotion. For the first time, Kaito really felt like a hero.

"Th-thank you."

His heart pounding, Kaito took a slice of his own creation. It was the first pizza he had ever baked in his life... What would it taste like?

"Ooh! That's good!"

His exclamation was abrupt, as the deliciousness filled his mouth.

The first thing to reach his taste buds was the cheese, which had mingled with the olive oil. The rich flavor soon gave way to the acidity of the tomato sauce. And finally, there was the aromatic snap of the parjee. The crust smelled wonderful and was also fluffy. The salt gave it just the right amount of bite. Kaito was no elf, but he had to agree that this was the most delicious pizza he'd ever tasted.

"Ow! It's hot! But so good!" He must have been even more starved than he'd realized, because he could hardly stop his hand as it went back for slice after slice. Before he knew it, he'd eaten an entire pizza.

"Ahhh... The sour tomato sauce, the sweetness of the cheese, and the smell of the parjee all come together, and it's just... It's just beautiful..."

The traces of flavor lingering in his mouth and his full belly inspired genuine happiness.

*This is it... This is what I've always wanted to eat.*

The elves were now merrily toasting each other, their faces a much healthier color.

*Calories, huh? Better be careful...*

"I'll be opening a pizza parlor, so, everyone, please feel free to stop by!!"

And with that, Kaito felt the joyous response emanating from the crowd.

## Kaito Treats the Headman's Household to Pizza

"Ow, ow, ow, ow..."

When he woke up the next morning, Kaito found himself groaning and cradling his arms. He'd made an awful lot of pizza the day before, and his muscles hurt. He could barely move.

"Goodness, Kaito, are you all right?" Fiona asked when she saw him rising unsteadily to his feet.

"Lord Kaito! Whatever is wrong?!" Lilia rushed to his side. Kaito managed a smile for her benefit.

"We did a lot of baking yesterday. I'm just a little sore..."

The pizza skill card had given him the knowledge of an experienced practitioner but not the body.

"That's terrible!!" Lilia dashed across the room and grabbed a first-aid kit.

"I don't think we need to—"

"You should keep them cool!!"

Kaito decided not to argue as Lilia bandaged him. He certainly wouldn't mind a little relief. Lilia took something like ointment and covered it in gauze, then wrapped it around Kaito's arms. Kaito found that her diligent attention gave him a surprisingly warm feeling.

*Gee, it's awful nice having someone to fuss over you like this. When you live by yourself, you have to deal with all your illnesses and injuries on your own...*

"How's that?" Lilia looked up at him, having finished applying the bandages.

Up close like this, Kaito could see how big and beautiful her emerald-like green eyes really were. Her strawberry-blond hair reflected the sunlight, shimmering gracefully.

*A girl this gorgeous is kind of wasted on me. Even if she does have an insane appetite...*

He decided it would be best not to push himself until he was more accustomed to the work. His arms felt like overinflated swim wings, like they might burst at any minute.

"Perhaps you should take today off?" Fiona offered, looking worried.

"You're right, but we have the oven going and everything..." He didn't want to waste the leftover heat. "I can manage a little bit." Then an idea struck him. "Um, if it's all right, would you let me make dinner tonight? You've taken such good care of me, I'd like to treat you to some pizza."

"We'd be very grateful...but please don't overexert yourself."

Kaito nodded vigorously at Edmond. "I'll be all right! Pizza for five, then!"

✳

Kaito was excited as he arrived at his shop. He wouldn't be baking until that night, but preparations had to start first thing in the morning. It took time to ferment the dough and especially to heat the oven.

"Hmm, a peel and brush for cleaning..." He read off the names of the new cards that had been added to his item pouch. He was grateful that he kept getting more items at each new stage, even if it was only because it was so early in his career.

He opened the oven door and used the peel to clean out the ash and cinders inside.

"Ow, ow, ow..."

"Oh, I'll do that," Lilia offered. She was becoming a genuinely helpful partner.

"Thanks. Could you clean up the embers in there?"

"Leave it to me!!" Lilia began moving the brush enthusiastically. A cloud of ash puffed up and assaulted their faces.

"Urgh...*cough, cough*!!"

Kaito helplessly broke into a coughing fit.

"*Hrkcoughcoughcough*!!"

Lilia, too, choked from the smoke.

"Yikes..." Kaito hurriedly opened the windows and door to let in fresh air. "Lilia...*cough*...go slow, okay?"

"*Hrkcoughhrk*... I'm very sor— *Hkkkcoughcoughcough!*"

She had gotten a little overexcited, that was all. She was a good person, albeit a bit scatterbrained and slightly rough around the edges.

"Look, now you've got dirt on your face." Kaito wiped away the smudges on Lilia's cheek.

"!!"

His heart rate jumped when he felt the smoothness of her skin, and he quickly looked away. "Uh, anyway, I'll handle the rest!!"

Eventually, they succeeded in cleaning the oven. Kaito picked out some small pieces of wood and started a fire.

"All right, oven's ready to go!" He picked up his item pouch. "Now ingredients..." He reached into the bag. He had used up all the ingredients his cards had provided the day before.

"Phew..." Several new cards had appeared in the bag. All were ingredients. "*Wheat Flour, Natural Yeast, Tomatoes.*" One by one, they appeared as he read them aloud. It amused him to see Lilia watching this with wide eyes. He felt a bit like he'd become a magician.

"Hmm? Garlic?" It was the first time he'd seen that ingredient. A moment later, different varieties of pizza suddenly popped into his head. "Tomato sauce plus garlic equals...marinara!!"

"Marinara?"

Lilia looked puzzled. "What kind of pizza is that?"

"It has the longest history of any Neapolitan pizza, having been created around 1750! It's a simple pie beloved by fishermen, featuring tomato sauce and garlic!"

Kaito couldn't lie to himself this time: He was dying to put his skills to use! But despite his burning passion, he realized he had gone over Lilia's head.

"Oh, sorry. That's knowledge from the world I used to be in. I know it doesn't mean much to you."

"No, it's fine..." Lilia gently wiped her hand with her mouth. *Drool...* "Just listening to you makes it sound good..."

"O-oh, does it?" Lilia had the look of a wild animal hunting its prey. "Well, I'm glad you're looking forward to it."

"Yes, I'm looking forward...to tonight..."

"Wait, Lilia, stop!! You can't eat a whole bulb of garlic!! I haven't even peeled it yet!!"

He practically had to jump on her to keep her from consuming the raw ingredients she'd picked up.

"Oh! I'm sorry! I just forgot myself..."

*Forgot yourself and almost ate an entire unpeeled bulb of garlic??*

"This isn't cooked yet! It wouldn't taste good this way!! I'll make plenty of food, so just calm down, Lilia!!"

"Okay..." Lilia nodded sweetly, but she continued eyeing the garlic.

"I'm making this pizza to show my gratitude to you guys! So I'll make it by myself! You just wait inside, okay?"

"Are you sure...?"

Kaito grabbed Lilia's hand as it reached for the garlic again. "I'm sure! Please just wait!"

"O-okay, I will!!" Having him take her hand inspired a fit of blushing and gaze aversion. "I'll wait like a good girl."

"Yes! Please do!!"

When he had finally succeeded at getting Lilia out of the kitchen, Kaito heaved a sigh of relief. Her "beast mode," her unfettered displays of appetite, worried him more than a little. How could such a restrained and quiet girl go so out of control when she got hungry?

Kaito finally got around to working on the meal.

\*

"All right, time to bake some pizzas!" It was almost dinner, and Kaito entered the pizza parlor, bubbling. He shaped the dough and got the tomato sauce ready. Because pizza marinara, unlike margherita, doesn't use cheese, he made sure there was plenty of sauce. He applied it in a spiral shape, remembering that inconsistency was key to delightful mouthfeel.

Then came a pinch of salt, followed by something called hanahakka, which was what he'd found in the garden to substitute for oregano.

Finally, he added the most important ingredient for good pizza marinara, the garlic. He put garlic slices onto the crust to bring out the aroma. He doused everything in olive oil, and the pizzas were ready to go.

"All right!" These were his first pizzas marinara, but he was very pleased with them. It was impossible not to smile as he looked at the rich pies, each as red as the setting sun. He put four of them into the oven, one after another. Cooking several at once was no problem for him. He lifted each one with the peel to check that it was done, then took them out.

"Ahhh, it smells so good!!" Kaito took the four pizzas straight to the mansion, wanting everyone to enjoy them fresh from the oven.

"Ah, Lord Kaito!!" His three dinner guests were already at the table and waiting anxiously. The table was set; all he had to do was provide the food.

"Here you go! My very first marinaras!!"

Lilia and her family all exclaimed as he set the pizzas on the table.

"Wow! It's so red, it looks like the setting sun!!" Lilia gushed admiringly. "It's such a rich color... What are those little black spots?"

"Hanahakka. For fragrance."

"It does smell wonderful..."

"I think it'll go well with the garlic. Go ahead—help yourselves!"

"Don't mind if we do!" The four of them immediately dug into the pizza.

"Mmmmm..." A satisfied sigh seemed to come from everyone at once.

"Oooh... The sour flavor of the tomatoes really spreads through your mouth."

"That garlic has a punch. It really brings out the taste!"

"The crust is so...so fluffy!"

All of them ate voraciously, and in no time at all, their plates were empty.

"Ahhh..."

Everyone at the table was clearly very happy. For a beautiful moment, they savored the aftertaste of the food on their palates.

Kaito felt the same way he had the day before; having people compliment the food he put so much effort into making felt even better than he'd originally thought.

*All right, I'll make this again!* thought Kaito, feeling motivated.

"Phew! I'm stuffed," Edmond said, wiping his mouth with a napkin. "Thank you!"

"I'll bring tea and some gelatin for dessert." Fiona bustled around the table, picking up dishes and setting out cups.

"Ahhh, what a pleasure to share a meal with my family."

"It certainly is."

"And it's so nice to have a new family member like this!"

"Thanks...I think." *What does that even mean?* Kaito worried. Was he *like* family? Or was he actually part of the family? That was the question.

*Geez. I'm getting so worked up, I'm starting to sound like Hamlet.*

"Enjoy, everyone!"

"Don't mind if I do." Kaito took his serving of gelatin Fiona had brought out and dug in. "Ahhh, that's so refreshing." The gelatin felt cleansing in his mouth. "Is this mint?"

"It's menthe and lemon."

Whatever menthe was, it was apparently a fresh-smelling herb similar to mint.

"The sweetness comes from extract of Sweet Slime."

"Huh? Slime?!" Kaito stared at the gelatin in disbelief.

"Yes," Fiona said matter-of-factly. "It has a lot of nutrients that make it an excellent beautifier." *Like collagen, perhaps. That's an alternate world for you...*

"Well, it's delicious."

"Thank you."

It wasn't especially sweet, but it was a perfect chaser for the pizza.

The headman's dining room was full of pictures and knickknacks.

Kaito's eye stopped on a garland of dried flowers, blue and white blossoms woven into a ring, and he pointed to it.

"What's that?"

"Ah, that's the flower garland my wife and I used at our wedding."

"We dried and saved it as a memento."

"Wow..."

*So they wore that on their head?* It was true the blue and white flowers had an innocent, pure aesthetic that would be well suited to a wedding.

"In our village, it's tradition for the groom to pick blue and white flowers for the bride."

"Then he gives the bride the garland as a gift, and she wears it at their wedding."

"Those flowers are called bluebells and whitebells. They only grow on sheer mountain cliffs, so they're not easy to get."

"That's what makes it such a touching gift."

"Huh..."

*Sounds like a real rite of passage. I wonder if it's anything like bungee jumping?*

Kaito was about to ask the question aloud but caught himself. Even he could tell it wasn't quite the same thing.

"You'll go pick them, too, won't you Kaito? For Lilia?"

"Er..."

Fiona sounded like she thought everything was already settled, and it brought Kaito up short. The entire family looked at him with hopeful eyes.

*Whoooa, I let my guard down for one minute, and look what happens! This is bad... This is real bad!*

Kaito began looking anywhere but at the people around him. "Oh!"

"Yes?"

"What's that? That, uh, pretty, shield-like thing?"

He directed their attention to something that appeared to be a shield but was the color of an iridescent beetle. The greenish shimmer was unlike anything he'd ever seen before.

"Ah, my dear Kaito, what excellent taste you have!" Edmond was nodding happily, to Kaito's relief. Apparently, he'd succeeded in changing the subject.

"That...is a dragon's scale."

"A dragon? There are dragons around here?"

Kaito thought for a moment that maybe they were teasing him, but everyone's faces turned serious, starting with Edmond's.

"There certainly are." He said it as though this were a perfectly obvious fact, but Kaito was dumbfounded.

*Sure, okay. When you've got a place with elves and slimes, I guess it only makes sense to have dragons, too. But still...dragons! Are they really huge creatures that fly through the sky and breathe fire?*

"Are there any around here?"

"One lives just past Twin Peak. He spends most of his time asleep, but he does wake up every once in a while."

"Twin Peak...?"

"That mountain with two summits that you can see to the east."

"Oh, is that it...?"

Kaito knew which mountain Edmond was talking about; it was pretty distinctive. It was quite a ways off, but not so far that a dragon couldn't fly there and back. To think there was a dragon so close by...

"Um...does he ever attack villages, perchance...?"

"Mm, well, it seems food has been scarce in the mountains lately, so he does make his way to inhabited areas sometimes..."

"Does he eat people?!"

"No, but he attacks the livestock and occasionally makes a mess of our fields."

"......"

It sounded a bit like on Earth when a bear woke up from hibernation and wandered into a town. And it wasn't unheard of for them to attack humans.

"Um, you seem pretty calm about this. If you don't mind my asking, isn't it a problem?"

"Of course it is. We wish we could do something about it, but the dragon is huge and terrible."

"What *do* you do when he comes?"

"Often, we get everyone in the village to make as much noise as they can in hopes of driving the creature off. We certainly couldn't win in a fair fight, so we try not to attack him directly. In a worst-case scenario, we might have to summon soldiers from the palace, but the warriors in our army aren't exactly very intimidating..."

"......"

Kaito hadn't realized the elves faced such a terrible situation. But then again, nobody seemed unduly worried about it. The damage it did wasn't awful, and they had no way to fight it... The dragon was more like a natural disaster than a monster.

"It's not all bad, though. Dragons naturally shed their old scales, and those are quite valuable. It gives us a chance to make a little money. That particular scale has been passed down in this family for generations."

"Wow..."

"Dragon scales are very tough and last a long time. That's what makes them precious."

"I see." Kaito's interest was piqued by talk of something so unique to an alternate world. "Is dragon meat...tasty, by any chance?" He was surprised to hear himself blurt out such a question.

Becoming the High-Calorie Hero seemed to have given him a bent for all things culinary.

"There are stories. Some claim that eating dragon meat makes you immortal. Others say just one mouthful contains enough poison to annihilate an entire village. Honestly, I've never heard of anyone actually eating dragon meat, so who knows?"

"Huh..."

There were obviously a lot of things Kaito didn't yet know about this world, many of them edible. It made him hungry to find out more.

# CHAPTER 6

# The Hero's Greatest Admirer, Hans the Woodcutter

After breakfast the next morning, Kaito and Lilia headed to the pizza parlor. The morning air was clean and bracing, and it promised that work to come would be a pleasure.

"All right! Gotta take care of the oven first."

"I'll help you!" Lilia once again offered her assistance.

"I appreciate it, but go slow, okay?" Kaito reminded her, still remembering the previous day's trouble.

"Gentle! Got it!!" Lilia picked up the cleaning peel.

"No, no!! I didn't mean *move* slowly. I just want you to *brush* slowly!! I wasn't asking you to move one centimeter per second or whatever!!"

Lilia always kept things interesting, at least.

When the cleaning was done, Kaito went to get the fire started and noticed they were running low on wood.

"Erk, not a lot of firewood here..."

"Let's ask Hans the woodcutter, then. He'll bring us some."

Kaito was a bit surprised by this. "So there's a woodcutter around here, huh?"

He asked Lilia to arrange the delivery while he started making the dough. They still had leftover ingredients.

Come to think of it, would he keep getting new ingredients forever? If it turned out he would only be given supplies early on, he'd eventually need to find a way to get them on his own.

That meant he needed money.

As Kaito worked the dough, trying to think of ways to come up with some cash, there was a knock on the door.

"Good morning! Hans the woodcutter, at your service! I brought firewood!"

"Wow, that was quick!"

When Kaito opened the door, he found a blue-eyed, curly-haired elf standing there. Or at least, he was pretty sure it was an elf. He had blond hair and pointy ears, but Hans was a little different from the other elves Kaito had met. For starters, he had a face as round as a rice ball. Lilia and the other elves of the village had much slimmer features. And then there was his physique. Most of the locals were noticeably thin, but Hans had a certain plumpness... In fact, he was about the shape of a barrel. His clothes looked fit to burst, like the buttons might fly off at any moment.

"Pleased to meet you! The headman sent me. I'm the woodsman Hans."

"Oh, nice to meet you, Hans." It seemed Hans was indeed a member of the village. In other words, definitely an elf... Probably.

Hans, for his part, seemed oblivious to Kaito's confusion. "You don't know how overjoyed I am to be talking to the hero himself!"

"O-oh yeah? Thanks..."

Hans had suddenly gotten so close that they were practically nose to nose. Kaito hurriedly put some distance between them.

*This guy is so intense it's scary!*

Hans was smiling happily and unloading a huge bundle of firewood from his back.

"Here's your delivery, as requested. Material from broad-leaved trees, not too smoky and doesn't leave a lot of soot."

"Thank you very—"

"Oops!"

Just as Kaito was trying to express his gratitude, the heavy wood threw Hans off-balance. The whole load clattered onto the floor in an avalanche, leaving Hans lying dazed on top. There was a further cracking sound as several of the logs gave way under Hans's weight. It was a cruel way of adding insult to injury.

"......"

"I'm sorry! I'm so sorry! I'm so very sorry!" Hans struggled to get up off the pile of wood. He was so round, it couldn't have been easy for him to stand.

"No, no, it's all right."

The poor woodcutter had gone so pale that Kaito felt downright sorry for him.

*He's...very emotional, isn't he?*

"I'm just so careless! I'm so very, very sorry!"

"No, seriously, don't worry about it."

At that moment, Hans looked directly at Kaito. His eyes brimmed with such passion that Kaito thought, *Is he about to confess his love for me or something?!*

Instead, Hans murmured, "I'm so happy you deigned to choose our world, O Honored Hero..."

"Huh...?"

*So...not a confession of love.*

That was a relief. Kaito stopped looking for a window he could jump through and turned his attention back to the elf.

"We prayed and prayed to the goddess, but she said something about heroes having a certain amount of discretion... And none of them ever picked us."

"......"

"That's why I'm so glad you're here!"

*Nu-uh, no way! I didn't pick this place! It looked like I had a choice, but I didn't! I got duped! Who would* want *to be the "High-Calorie Hero"?!*

But, he reflected, he'd never realized the goddess might have had a reason like that for sending him.

"I waited eagerly to find out what sort of person might come for us, but when I saw you, Lord Kaito, I was so overwhelmed that I wept like a boy!"

"Oh... Uh..."

Had the elves' hopes really been that high? True, they had seemed awfully excited to see him.

*I wonder if I can really be the person they want me to be...*

"A young man from a foreign land, with exotic black hair and eyes. And such a kind heart! And no sooner did you arrive than you introduced us to that wonderful food you call pizza..." Hans was visibly quaking with emotion.

Kaito felt a stab of guilt.

*I... I'm sorry. I didn't exactly choose this place, and I didn't do it because I was eager to save your world. I just kind of...wound up here, making pizza... But I'm gonna give this everything I've got, so forgive me!!*

Kaito couldn't break Hans's heart, so he swallowed his words.

"I don't think I saw you at the welcome party..." There had been a lot of people there, but Hans would have made an impression in the crowd of slim, elegant elves.

"No, sir! I was very eager to go and welcome you, but in my excitement, I took a fall down the stairs and couldn't move for a while! But I'm fine now!"

Hans took a large glass jar out of the bag hanging from his shoulder. There was something golden inside. The woodcutter pulled out a spoon and began chowing down on it.

Somewhat concerned about what was happening, Kaito asked hesitantly, "What's...that...?"

"It's honey! Do you want some, too, O Honored Hero?"

"Oh, no, thanks..." He didn't think he could manage mouthfuls of the thick, gooey honey without anything to put it on. But Hans happily emptied the jar.

"Phew! Energizing! Now to gather up this firewood!"

*I think I know now why Hans is the only fat elf...*

Hans noticed Kaito staring at his rotund belly and said, "Ah, changed your mind about the honey, have you? Don't worry—I've got more!" He produced a veritable pile of glass jars, all full of honey. So that was why his bag looked so stuffed.

"Nonononono! How much of that stuff do you have anyway?!"

"The idea of running out of honey is the most terrifying thing I can imagine..."

"Are you an addict? You've got a honey addiction!!"

"*Ad-dict?* Is that something tasty?" Hans's eyes were shining.

"Um, let's get away from the subject of food for a minute... You know what? Never mind. You live your life however you want..."

"...? Yes, sir!" Hans cheerfully began collecting the firewood. "Oh yeah, I was thinking I'd make a sign for you if you wanted. I've got a board with me, if you'd like."

"A sign?" True, if he was going to have a shop, a sign would be nice.

"What are you going to call this place?"

"Huh? You mean its name?"

He hadn't even thought about it.

*That's a good point. A restaurant needs a name... But I just can't think of one on the spot like this!*

"You two, brainstorm something!"

"I know!!" Lilia immediately raised her hand.

"Yes?"

"How about 'Delicious Pizza'?!"

Kaito had hoped she really had something, but he practically fell out of his chair at this suggestion.

*Keep it together. Big smile.*

"...Uh, yeah, thank you. It's certainly simple and direct, but it doesn't really say *restaurant name* to me. It's more...exposition."

"I see!"

Lilia began thinking deeply. Hans's hand shot up.

"Got a good idea?"

"Yes, sir!"

Hans opened his mouth to speak, his expression tense.

"Pizzero!"

"...Pizzero?" Kaito stared at Hans for a moment. *Yep, he's keeping a straight face. He must be serious.* "...Did you just put *pizza* and *hero* together...?"

"Yes!!"

"Hmm. Yeah... Like what they used to do with light novel titles. But don't you think it's a little cryptic?"

"Would longer be better? Then how about 'The Shop Where the Honored Hero Makes the World's Very Best Pizza Ever'?"

"...Uh, yeah. That definitely lets you know what you're getting into...

but I think it's a little too long. It might be hard to remember. Or say. Y'know?"

*This is getting us nowhere. Yep, it's my fault for relying on others. What to do, what to do...?*

Kaito sank deep in thought.

The name of his pizza parlor had to be something distinctive, elegant, with a good sound, but memorable.

Then it struck him:

*How about 'Grateful World's-End Pizza'?*

*Magnificent pizza at the world's end.*

*Yeah, that sounds good. That sounds cool.*

"Ahem..."

But just as he was about to share his idea with Lilia and Hans, he remembered the faces of the elves when he'd announced his made-up hero name. They'd been completely flummoxed. Their reaction had been almost physically painful to him, and now he was on the verge of a repeat performance...

*What was I thinking? This isn't the end of the world! It's just a normal village. 'Grateful Another-World Pizza,' then? Because, hey, I'm in an alternate world. Nah, that doesn't sound remotely appetizing. It would only leave people wondering what was in my pies...*

"What's wrong, O Honored Hero?" Hans was looking at him with concern.

"Oh, nothing... Simple is best, you know? I think I need to go back to basics."

Kaito started racking his brain. *I need a name that's easy but could only belong to my shop. Something inviting. Something that'll make people confident the food is gonna be delicious.*

"What about...'The Hero's Pizza Parlor'?"

*I'm the only hero in this world. Or...the only one who makes pizza, anyway. So that makes the name unique. But is it a little too simple...?*

Kaito's heart pounded as he gauged the elves' reaction.

"That's fantastic!!"

"I knew you would come up with something, Lord Kaito!!" Hans and Lilia trembled in sheer admiration.

"Y-you really like it?"

"It's the best!"

"I knew you could do it, Lord Kaito!"

It felt pretty good, having the two of them heap praise on him like this, but he couldn't help wondering if he'd really come up with something worthy of this level of adulation. Still, it was simple and understandable, and that was what counted.

"Well, time to make the sign, then!" Hans pulled out some wood-working tools.

*That is one versatile bag...*

Kaito hadn't seen woodworking implements for a long time, and it pulled on his heartstrings. He remembered how they used to make desks and stuff in class.

*Hey, isn't this kind of dangerous? That wood is hard; he won't be able to keep his hand steady...*

"Yipe!" Hans was smoothing the surface of the board with a chisel-like tool when his hand slipped.

"Yeeeek!" Kaito gave a shriek.

"No worries—I'm okay."

"'Okay'?! You almost chopped off your finger!" Kaito's heart was still pounding. He'd nearly witnessed a major emergency before his very eyes.

"No worries at all!"

*Scrape.* This time the hand holding the chisel slipped slightly, and the sharp blade grazed Hans's protruding stomach.

"Eeek!" *I can't do it! I can't watch!* "Hans, stop! Just forget about the sign!!"

"No worries! I'm just gonna carve the name in here..."

*Krack!*

"Hrrk!"

This time the blade bit into the wood inches away from his thumb.

"Huh? This isn't quite working..."

"Hans! Wait, Hans! Hans, Hans!!" Kaito couldn't help shouting.

"What is it?"

"You almost buried that thing in your hand!"

"I'm fine."

"You are not fine!"

*I can't do it. This is too awful to watch. Plus, I don't want a sign that's covered in blood! What can I do, what can I do...?*

"Hans! I've got a request!"

Hans looked up at him. "Anything!"

*Now, what can I say to distract him...? Huh? What's this feeling of déjà vu...? Oh. Lilia. Lilia was a handful, too, in her own way.*

"Um, why don't you let me carve it?"

"Oh, no! I'll take care of it!"

"But, uh, it's my sign for my store, so maybe I should do it."

Hans still didn't look happy.

Kaito thought hard. *He wants to help me. It's painfully obvious. But it's backfiring on him.*

"I just need you to help me out."

Hans looked doubtful. "Help you out how...?"

"Start eating some of that honey. You know, the stuff in your bag."

"How will that help...?" Hans still hadn't relinquished his grip on the chisel.

*It really won't. This is a stupid idea.*

"You get so energized when you're eating that honey that it makes me feel strong just watching. That's how you're helping."

"Oh, I get it!"

Kaito wasn't sure exactly what Hans "got" about his incoherent excuse, but the elf happily began cramming honey into his mouth.

"Is everyone around here like this...?" Kaito muttered as he took up the chisel.

✳

At long last, Kaito finished the sign. His work had been halting and slow at first, but by the time he was finished, it was going along smoothly.

*Hey, I'm pretty handy.*

"Phew... Done!!"

"Phew... Done!!"

Just as Kaito finished the sign, Hans finished eating the honey.

*Looks like I just made it...*

"Nice work, Hans!! With your help, I was able to get the sign done!"

"And done well! It looks wonderful."

"Well, it was all thanks to you."

*Thanks to you keeping out of the way, specifically...*

"It is an honor to be of service to you, O Honored Hero!!"

Hans's eyes were welling up with emotion.

"Y-yeah..."

*Even though I did most of the actual carving...and you just sat there eating honey.*

Kaito was completely exhausted, but he managed a smile. The unfamiliar work had left his muscles stiff and his stomach empty.

"Let me treat you to a pizza to thank you."

So this was the situation: Hans had caused nothing but trouble, so Kaito was going to treat him to a pizza.

"Wow, really?!"

"Yeah. I'm pretty hungry, myself. How about you, Lilia?"

Lilia nodded vigorously.

When he saw the margherita pizza that Kaito cooked up, Hans howled, "Woooooooooooowwwie!! Does that ever look good! Look at that melting cheese...!!"

It occurred to Kaito that this was the first time Hans would have encountered this pizza. "Get it while it's hot!"

Staring at the dish, Hans slapped his knee in an epiphany. "I'll bet this would go great with honey!"

"Huh?"

*Honey? Like...honey honey?*

Yes indeed. Hans eagerly pulled out a bottle.

"I keep an emergency jar around for situations just like this!"

"What the heck?!"

"Bon appétit!" And then Hans was slathering honey all over the pizza.

*I've seen people put Tabasco sauce on their pizza, but honey?!*

"Hans, wait—! Hans—!" Kaito's voice was practically cracking.

"This is amaaaaazing!!" Hans quivered with emotion. "The beeeeest!!

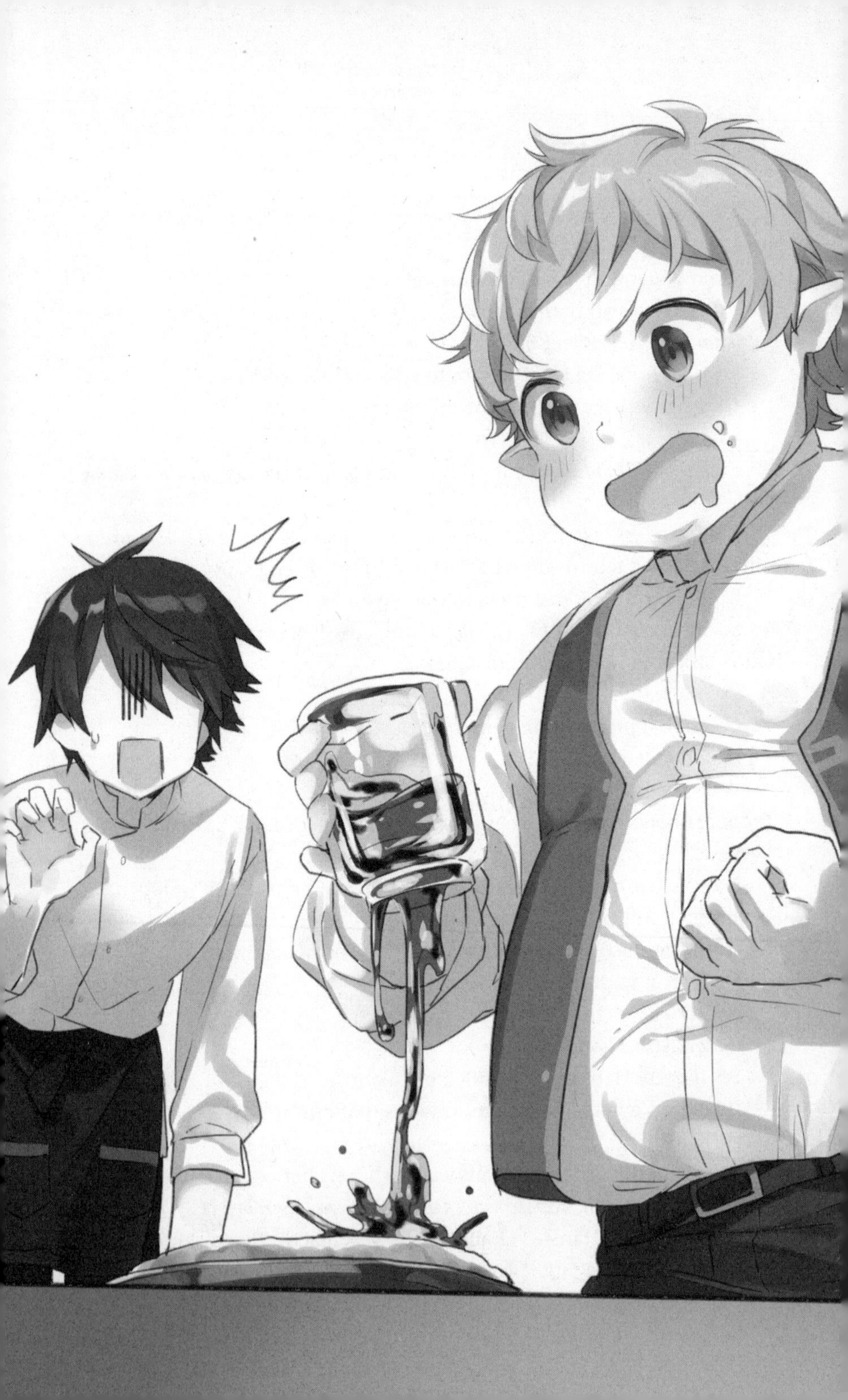

Ahhh, the cheese and the honey just melt together! And the way it complements the distinctiveness of the tomato sauce—!"

"Oh... Oh really...?"

*Could the tastes actually go together?*

"I put honey on everything I eat!" He made Kaito think of the kind of people who drenched everything they ate in mayo.

*So some things stay the same no matter what world you're in...*

"Do you want some, Honored Hero?"

Hans the honey freak held out a slice to Kaito. Rich, dewy honey was dripping from it.

*It actually looks sort of nice. But...*

"I'll pass, thanks. You can have all of it."

*...I'm getting heartburn just looking at it. Just how much of a honey freak is this guy?!*

Kaito patted himself on the back for not asking the question out loud.

And so what was supposed to be a simple firewood delivery turned into a messy, all-day affair. But at least he got a sign out of it. He was looking forward to hanging it the next day.

# CHAPTER 7

# Kaito's First Delivery Customer Is a Career Woman

"Lord Kaitoooooo!!"

Kaito was cleaning the oven the next morning when Lilia burst in, throwing the door open so hard that it slammed against the wall. She had clearly been running full tilt; her hair was a mess.

"What's going on, Lilia?"

The elf girl's green eyes were shining. "We got an order!!"

"What?!"

"Someone wants a pizza delivered!!"

"All right!" Their first delivery customer. Kaito's heart raced. "Who is it? What kind of person are they? What kind of pizza do they want?"

"Calm down, Lord Kaito," Lilia said, smiling at his excitement. "The order is from a person named Belinda."

"A woman, huh?"

"Yes! She's extremely smart. She even studied in another country once, and now she works as the queen's tutor at the castle."

"Woooow, amazing!"

*So a career woman, huh?*

"Her house is about five minutes away by carriage."

"Carriage?!"

Now that he thought about it, Kaito realized he'd neglected to figure out how he would make deliveries. Doing them on foot around here didn't seem feasible. He wanted the pizza to be as fresh as possible when it got to the customers.

"You mean carriage, like…"

"Oh, you can use the family's carriage. Though it's more of a cart… It doesn't have a roof."

"That would be great!"

It felt like he had to rely on the headman's family for everything. *I've got to make sure I get this place up and running and stand on my own two feet.*

"Uh, by the way, I don't know how to…drive?…pilot?…a carriage…"

"Oh, I can drive it."

"Thank you so much…!!"

Lilia was turning out to be a huge help. She could knead dough and clean the oven, and now it turned out she could drive a carriage.

*She's really a good girl…and pretty cute, too.*

Kaito hurriedly dismissed the thought. He had a delivery to focus on.

"So what kind of pizza does she want? All I can really do right now are margherita and marinara…"

"She said she wants to try them both… But there's only one of her, and she can't eat two whole pizzas. Whatever shall we do?" Lilia asked, confused.

"We put them both on one pie…half and half!!"

"Half and half…?" Lilia's eyes were wide.

"It's very popular for deliveries. Good for people who get bored with just one flavor or who want to try two different things. Half of it will be margherita, and half will be marinara!"

"Can you do that?!" Lilia gasped in shock.

"You have to keep a close eye on the cooking time, but sure."

"Amazing! That's incredible, Lord Kaito!" Lilia was so full of praise that Kaito found himself getting a bit embarrassed.

*Anybody in my country could have told you about that…*

"Okay, let's get started!!"

"I'll get the carriage ready!!" Lilia left the restaurant, and Kaito set about making the pizza. Both flavors used tomato sauce as a base, so the first step was the same. Kaito put a spiral of tomato sauce on the shaped crust.

Now it was time to show what he could do. First, he put mozzarella cheese and parjee on exactly half of the pizza. The other half got a dash of salt and some hanahakka, along with some sliced garlic. Finally, he drizzled olive oil over the whole thing.

"Perfect!" He slid the finished pizza onto the peel and put it in the oven. Because both halves had different ingredients, careful cooking time would be essential. Kaito diligently rotated the pie, making sure both sides got cooked thoroughly.

"That ought to just about do it..."

The pizza came out perfect. Kaito put it on a dish and set a silver lid over it. That would help keep it warm.

"Liliaaaa!! It's all set!!"

Outside, Lilia was already aboard the carriage. The vehicle was pulled by a single white horse. The animal seemed to be from the elf village, a beautiful thoroughbred. The "carriage" was a simple construct of wooden boards, made for carrying cargo. Lilia waved, the reins in her hands.

"I'm ready!" Kaito jumped up next to her. "Now, off we go!!"

"Sure thing!"

Then the carriage was off. Lilia's speed was perfect, not too fast and not too slow. They weren't going much faster than a bicycle, so Kaito wasn't worried about sitting out in the open.

"You're really good at this, Lilia."

"I've been around horses and carriages my entire life!"

"Wow. Is that so...?"

Come to think of it, I've only ever seen them on television. It's a little wobbly, but the breeze sure is nice. This isn't bad at all.

"Are you a rider, Lord Kaito?"

"I've never been on a horse. Well, once, I guess. I did this pony ride once when I was a kid."

He had been at some amusement park. His memories of the ride were hazy. It had involved one of the staff members leading the horse around; Kaito had literally just been along for the ride.

"I wonder if I could learn..."

"I'm sure you could!! If you want, I could teach you."

"Thanks. I'd like that."

The carriage rattled along, and before they knew it, they were at Belinda's house. It was a small place, but the garden was well tended.

"Hello! Pizza delivery!"

The door opened immediately to reveal a woman in her late twenties (Kaito thought; he wasn't very good at guessing elf ages yet) wearing glasses. Her long chestnut-colored hair was tied back in a single bunch. Her almond-shaped eyes were olive green. She cut a rather stern-looking figure.

"Please come in." She ushered Kaito and Lilia into the parlor. It was covered in a subdued but girlish flowery pattern. "I'd like to chat with you a bit, so I'll put some tea on."

"Uh, sure." Kaito was a bit surprised. He'd expected to make the delivery and go right back home, but this was his first delivery customer. If possible, he wanted to observe her reaction and hear what she thought.

"Here you go." She offered him a cup with a cute golden flower on it. She even brought out a plate of cookies.

"Thank y—"

"Bon appétit!" Before Kaito could even express his gratitude, Lilia had shoved the cookies into her mouth. "Wow! Delicious! These have cornmeal in them, right?"

"Yes, that's right."

*A cornmeal cookie... I would've liked to try that...*

But the plate, previously home to four cookies, was empty.

*Lilia... You and your monster appetite...*

Lilia sipped her tea, completely oblivious to Kaito's dirty look.

"Well then, I'll help myself. Do you cut this before you eat it?" Belinda was holding a knife and fork.

"Oh, it's already cut into slices. Just pick one up."

She looked at Kaito in surprise. "Really? Pick it up?"

"Your hands might get a little dirty, but it's the easiest way to eat a pizza. Plus, it's delicious."

"...Well, all right." She sounded determined. She picked up a slice of margherita.

*I guess she probably comes from a good background. She's a little hesitant to eat with her hands.*

Belinda took a bite of the margherita, and her eyes went wide.

"......!!"

"How is it?"

"It's wonderful!! The cheese is so rich, and the crust is so fluffy!!"

When she had finished the slice, Belinda took a piece of the marinara.

"Ah! The sourness of the tomato sauce is perfect!! It goes so well with the garlic!!"

Kaito felt a rush of relief to see Belinda enjoying the food so much. Mission accomplished.

Belinda readily finished the entire pie, then wiped her mouth with a paper napkin.

"What did you think? Did you like it?"

"Well..." Belinda cocked her head in thought. "The margherita is extremely rich. It has an aggressive strength, like a wild animal that wants to drag you off. It's like being pulled by a big, muscular arm you just can't resist..."

"......"

Kaito stared at Belinda, dumbstruck.

*She is talking about pizza, right...?*

"The marinara is more like a cheerful man. Open and honest, but somehow cynical. He has a passionate heart and leads you gently along."

"......"

Belinda was rapturous.

*A man? Did she just compare a pizza to a man?*

That was when his eye wandered over to Belinda's bookshelf. Among the scores of difficult specialist tomes, several books with purple dust jackets stood out. A series of some type, it appeared.

"......!"

Kaito's eyes went wide as he happened to notice the titles.

*Dragged Away by a Beast in the Desert Night. The Kidnapped Fake Bride. The Secret of the Handsome Duke. In the Mansion of Delights...*

Unmistakably novels in the vein of Harlequin romances. Belinda, it seemed, enjoyed love stories, which influenced the way she described her pizza.

"Is something wrong?"

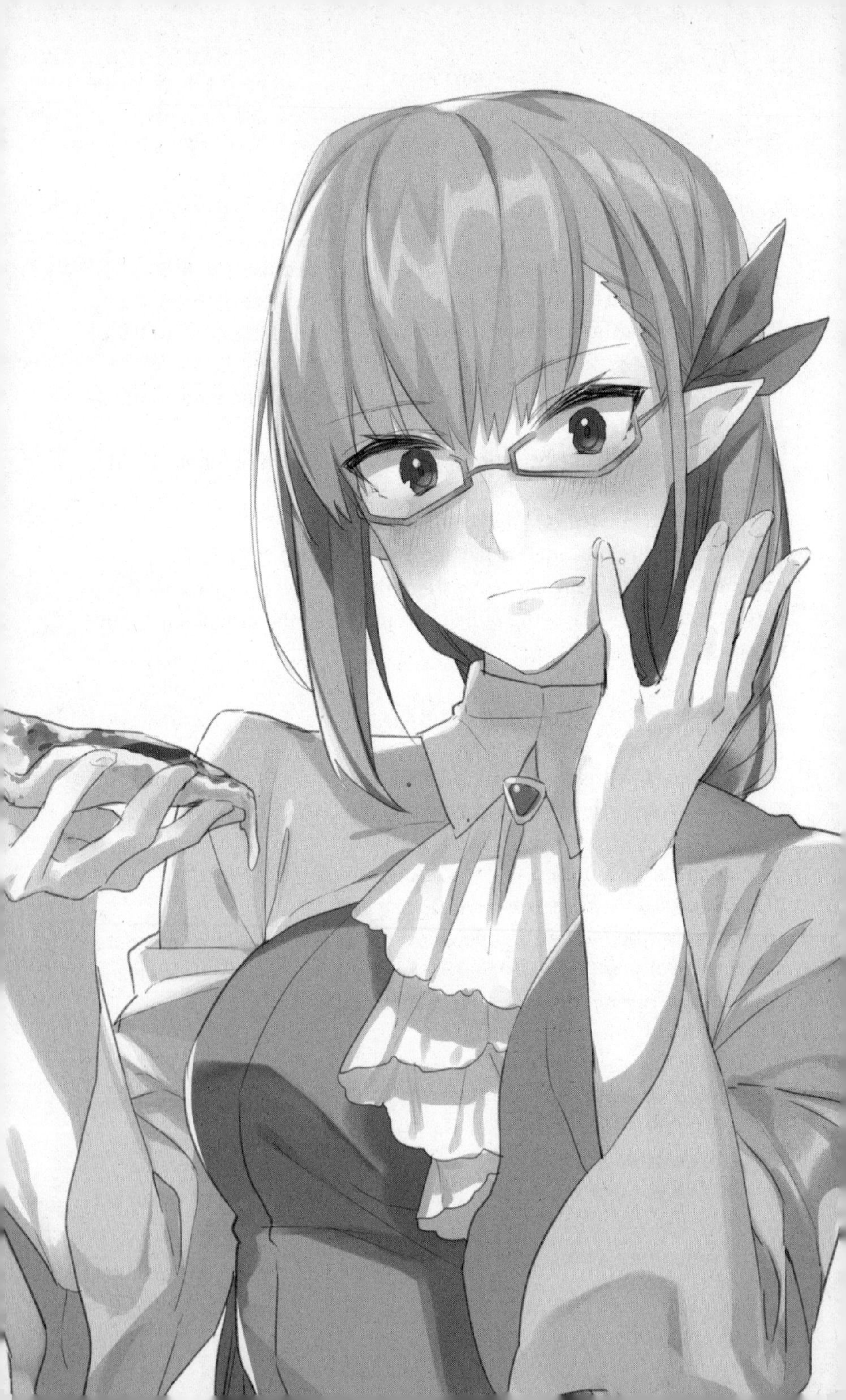

"Huh?" Kaito realized he had been staring fixedly at her bookshelf. Belinda was looking at him curiously. "Oh, uh, no. I was just thinking, you're quite a reader..."

Belinda heaved a sigh. "The cultural level in this nation is disappointingly low. It's not easy to get books. I have to wait for the Great Market each month to get anything."

"The Great Market? What's that?"

"On the first of every month, there is a market in the town square. Merchants from other countries often show up, so you can buy things that would normally be unavailable. It's quite a lively place."

"Huh..."

So ingredients weren't the only things lacking around here. Apparently, they were short on books and all sorts of things. He could see why they had been hoping for a hero.

"How do you intend to save this country now that you're here, Honored Hero?"

"Sorry...?"

"You did come to save our world, didn't you?"

"Well, I guess so..."

*I sure didn't* was something Kaito knew better than to say at that moment. Belinda was seriousness itself. Apparently, when she'd said she wanted to chat, she hadn't meant about the pizza.

"Look, I hate to disappoint you, but I'm really not that great a hero."

"......"

"The best I can do is to cheer everyone up by making some tasty pizza." She continued staring at him. "So it'd make me very happy if you would just enjoy my cooking and not worry too much about the whole saving-the-world thing."

"......"

Maybe she was disappointed.

Finally, Belinda opened her mouth. "At first, I didn't know what to think about you."

"Huh?"

"This country surely did need a hero. But welcoming an outsider into our quiet, peaceful nation... I worried you might upset things."

"Ohhh..."

Kaito exhaled. He hadn't realized some people felt that way.

"But your words were quite reassuring. Now I'm glad you came."

"Uh..."

"Our country isn't very eager for change or development. Many people are still trapped in the old ways. It's hard to break people out of those habits, but I believe a powerful, revolutionary figure like a hero might be able to help us." Belinda smiled at Kaito. "I'm confident you'll be able to introduce slow, subtle change."

Kaito had the distinct sense she was complimenting him. "Uh, thanks..."

"I'm sure I'll order another delivery in the future."

Since he had a willing customer right here, Kaito decided to do an informal survey. "I'm thinking about expanding our menu. Anything you'd like to see?"

"Good question..." Belinda thought for a moment. "I'd like there to be something sweet, perhaps."

"Something sweet..." *How very feminine.* He hadn't expected such a request from her. "Got it. I'll look into it."

"Please do."

*She's right, though. Leaflets for pizza places always include dessert. Not that I've ever ordered one.*

Belinda paid for her meal, and Lilia and Kaito left the house.

"She's...pretty impressive."

"Miss Belinda is very well known for her intelligence. She's always thinking about difficult things."

"Is that right?"

*It takes all kinds, I guess...*

Kaito was pleased by the discovery that he could meet different types of people through pizza. It made the job seem more meaningful than he'd first believed.

"...Are you thinking about Miss Belinda?"

"Huh?" Kaito, surprised by her soft voice, looked at Lilia, who sat holding the reins of the carriage.

"Miss Belinda is very beautiful, isn't she? I know smart, pretty women are attractive." She turned her head away and pouted.

*What is she pouting about? Whatever. I've got to get her back in a good mood.*

"Nice work today, Lilia! Thanks to you, our first delivery was a big success! When we get back to the house, I'll bake you a pizza to thank you!"

"......"

"Lilia?" His pulse was starting to quicken as Lilia stayed expressionless.

"...Make sure you put plenty of cheese on it."

"I sure will!!"

Seeing Lilia back in good spirits was a huge relief.

# CHAPTER 8

# Lilia's Girls' Day In

"There are some unsettling rumors going around..."

"Huh...?"

It was a breakfast like any other at Lilia's household when Edmond spoke darkly.

"They concern our queen, Her Majesty Eleonora..."

"Your queen, huh...?" The name didn't ring any bells for Kaito, but they were obviously talking about the most important person in the country.

"Yes. Last year, her parents passed away, and Her Majesty Eleonora inherited the rule of the kingdom at just sixteen years old. She had been raised for the throne from childhood and is both a capable and responsible person, but..."

Edmond seemed to be having trouble finishing his sentence.

"But? What about her?"

"It seems she doesn't think favorably of your pizza."

"What...?"

"Nutrition is something she takes almost as seriously as leadership. As a rule, she eats only vegetables and fruits. She claims that's the proper diet for elves."

"I see..."

*So, kind of a vegetarian. And maybe an...organic something-or-other?*

The implication was that she would regard calorie-heavy junk like pizza as a sin.

"What I mean to say is, forgive us. You've come as our hero, yet you haven't even been invited to the palace."

"Oh, uh, don't worry about it."

*I really don't care one way or the other about the palace.*

Edmond seemed very apologetic, but Kaito didn't especially like stiff, formal occasions. If the queen decided to try to shut him down by force, that would be a problem, but if she just didn't like his food, well, that was okay.

"Now, with that out of the way, I hear some of Lilia's friends will be coming over today. Is that right?"

"Yeah, we'll be borrowing the living room."

At Lilia's request, Kaito was going to treat three of her friends to pizza. Unfortunately, his restaurant wasn't yet equipped with a seating area, so they had to use the mansion's living room.

"...Lilia has truly found an excellent husband...," Edmond said, overcome with emotion. Kaito became flustered.

"Uh, I don't... I mean, I don't think we've actually gotten married yet..."

"Oh, yes, of course. You're both so young. There's no need to rush. Still, though, it does behoove you to keep a certain distance from other women. Observe propriety and all that."

"Um..."

*Isn't that basically the definition of being married...?*

But Kaito couldn't say anything because Edmond rolled right along. "I know! I know how it is! Hero of the land, exotic looks—every girl in the village must have eyes for you. It's enough to set a young man's head spinning!"

"Uh, not particularly—"

Kaito's sole concerns at the moment were what he had to accomplish in this world and how best to improve his pizza making.

"There's no need to hide it!" Edmond clapped Kaito on both shoulders. There was an unexpected sparkle in his eye, and his voice was passionate. "We men understand these things. A man is an eternal hunter!

But there's one quarry you mustn't pursue, and that's the friends of your wife-to-be. Only agony comes of it!" Edmond's face stiffened in a grimace of fear.

*Is he...speaking from experience?*

"Men always think they can hide these things, but it's a vain hope! Women have a sixth sense, a sharp intuition, and you'll soon be discovered. And then—misery!"

"Sir, I was definitely not thinking about getting anywhere near Lilia's friends..."

"Yes, of course. I knew you to be a loyal man the moment I saw you! Take good care of my Lilia."

"Huh?" Kaito stood dumbfounded, with the distinct sense that he had dug his hole even deeper than before.

"Well, have fun with the girls today. I have a meeting I must attend. See you!"

Kaito couldn't get a word out before Edmond had bustled from the room.

*Why won't anyone listen to me...?*

Kaito felt a wave of fatigue but headed for the shop nonetheless. He had to make pizza before company arrived.

"Ahhh, helloooooo!!"

"Thank you so much for having us today!!"

The girls greeted Kaito with voices that were veritable screeches to his ears, making no effort at all to hide their interest in him.

"Hello. Pleased to meet you."

"Goodness, we met at the welcome party!"

"Oh, but we haven't introduced ourselves yet, have we?"

"I'm Alisha."

"I'm Elizabeth."

"I'm Charlotte."

"Er, charmed..."

All of them had straight, long golden hair; frankly, he could hardly tell one from another. He managed to remember them, though, because Alisha was short, Elizabeth was tall, and Charlotte had a freckle on her nose.

"Okay, I'll cook the pizzas up and bring them in."

"We'll set the table. Oh, and this is from my parents. For the Honored Hero." Alisha held out a green vegetable that looked like spinach and something else that seemed like mushrooms. "We grew these in our own field."

"Thanks…" Kaito had been planning on making regular margheritas, but when he saw the proffered vegetables, he changed his mind.

*It might be interesting to try something a little different…*

"Oh, Lilia, here's some apple juice." Elizabeth took out some bottled juice while Charlotte produced a paper bag. "I brought paper napkins. Don't you think the owl design is cute? I found them at the Great Market last month."

The pitch of the girls' chatter rose quickly, and Kaito showed himself out. He might be in another world, and the girls might be elves, but the way they behaved didn't seem so different from gaggles of girls in his own world. Was this what they called a "girls' day in"? Kaito had never been a part of such a thing.

"Okay! Time to show these girls what I can do."

Kaito boiled the vegetables he'd received and sliced the mushrooms thinly. Then it was time to shape the crust. Judging by Lilia, those girls were likely to have massive appetites. They could probably devour a large pizza with no trouble. He decided to make five, including some for himself. He covered them with tomato sauce, then added the vegetables and mushrooms.

"I've got a good feeling about this!" Kaito began baking the pizzas one by one.

*

"Sorry to keep you waiting!"

As Kaito brought in the meal, Lilia and her friends rose in excitement to greet him.

"Woooow!!" No sooner was the food on the table than Lilia and her friends were cooing in admiration. "It looks wonderful!!"

"Are these flowers?"

"Yeah, they are. Can you see them?"

"I can!!"

Kaito had arranged the sliced mushrooms to look like petals and the boiled vegetables to look like stems and leaves. The happiness on the girls' faces told him it was a success.

"I thought I'd use the stuff from your garden right away. Thanks for bringing it, Alisha."

"Wow, I'm flattered!!" Alisha burst into a smile.

"What is this pizza called?"

"It's called pizza *capricciosa*. It basically means 'on the chef's whim.' I tried arranging the vegetables Alisha gave me into a flower shape."

"That's amaaaaaaaazing!!"

"Come on now, dig in."

The girls' ecstatic reactions made Kaito reflect once more on how important presentation was. Food was enjoyed with the eyes first—colors and shapes—before being put in the mouth. Get the appearance right, and people look forward to tasting it even more.

One by one, the girls erupted in praise.

"It's delicious!"

"Amazing! What a wonderful texture! The tomato sauce is so thick, and you can really sink your teeth into the vegetables. And of course, the crust is so fluffy. It's like there's more to discover with every bite you take!"

"I will never get tired of this!"

Kaito had gotten pretty confident in his pizza-making abilities, but the prospect of entertaining Lilia's friends had intimidated him somewhat. Now, at last, he felt his worries fading.

*Thank goodness...*

The girls gobbled up the large pizza.

"How are you doing? If you're still hungry, I can make more..."

"It's okay! If we eat any more, we won't have room for dinner."

"...Wow, you're still planning to have dinner?"

*So that huge pizza was just a snack? Ah, to be young again...*

It was then that Kaito noticed how lively the girls seemed. Their cheeks held a slight reddish tinge, and their skin seemed to be shining mildly. Maybe the delicious pizza had filled them with energy. At least, he would be happy to think so.

"I heard you were opening a restaurant."

"Yeah. Just takeout for now. We deliver! Be sure to let all your friends and neighbors know."

"How much does a pizza cost?"

"One silver coin."

He had determined the price after consulting with Edmond and his family. It was a bit expensive for a meal but, considering the ingredients involved, not too expensive. For the time being, Kaito was getting his ingredients from cards, but if the supply ever stopped flowing, this price would stand him in good stead. And since he was hoping to expand in the future, he would need funds.

"Sounds good. I'm sure I'll order something."

"Tea's on!" Drinks were brought out for the well-fed girls.

"Thank you very much!"

"Hey, I don't know too much about this world, but are you girls all in school?"

"Only the smartest kids go to the Academy of Higher Education. The entrance exams are really hard." Everyone nodded as Charlotte explained, "So I help in my family's orchard. Alisha works at her family's store."

"Alisha is the best at sewing! Her mom is a sewing teacher."

"We're all students of hers."

"I get it. You're all friends from class." Suddenly, something occurred to Kaito. Weren't these girls all the same age as the queen, Eleonora? "Have any of you ever met Queen Eleonora?"

"Sure. We pay our respects when she comes to the harvest festival and stuff."

"What's she like?"

Suddenly, the girls' faces were all beaming.

"She's sooooo pretty—"

"—and sooooo cool! Mature! You'd never think she was the same age as us!"

"Yeah! She's on another level!"

"I guess that's royalty for you."

Clearly, Eleonora was the object of some admiration.

"It sounds like she's got it rough, though… She had to take the throne so suddenly, and some people wonder if she'll be able to maintain our relations with the neighboring countries."

"Ah…"

A young, politically inexperienced girl thrown into the realm of international diplomacy? The other local rulers would eat her alive.

"Then again, we've never been a very powerful country, so maybe things won't change so much after all!"

"We're the smallest of all the nations around here, and the poorest, too!"

The girls were smiling as though none of this had much to do with them. Kaito gave a weak grin. True, the country of the elves wasn't flush with resources, but time flowed easily here. He could focus on making his pizzas and find a whole day over in the blink of an eye.

*I never expected to have moments like these.*

He'd hoped to be an awesome hero, but now he reflected on how difficult it would probably be if he were constantly having to fight. He would never get a calm moment, and all the responsibility would be on his shoulders. He would probably get hurt. People might die.

*Maybe making pizzas is more my speed.*

"So, Honored Hero." Alisha sounded teasing, but her eyes were full of curiosity. Kaito swallowed; he had a bad feeling about this. "How are things between you and Lilia?"

"Is it true you're going to get married?"

"You work together, don't you?"

The questions came flying at him, pinning Kaito in place. "Well, uh, you see…"

He glanced at Lilia, who had gone red with embarrassment and was stealing furtive glances at him.

"Uh, I have to go check on the oven!!"

"Oh, he ran off! He's so shy, that hero…"

"His face was completely red! Hey, so is Lilia's!"

Kaito could hear the girls' laughter behind him as he fled the mansion and headed for the shop.

# CHAPTER 9 Eleonora's Secret

Kaito was getting the oven ready one morning when the door of his restaurant flew open.

"Kaito! This is terrible!" It was Edmond, his face pale.

"What's going on? What's terrible?" Judging by the headman's pallor, it was clearly a pretty big deal.

"A messenger just arrived from the palace!"

"What? From the palace?"

That made Kaito's heart rate spike. He'd heard that Queen Eleonora, who lived at the palace, wasn't a big fan of pizza. What had she sent a messenger for? Did she mean to charge him with sedition and throw him in jail? A whole parade of awful images ran through his mind in the span of an instant.

"The messenger says you must bring a pizza to the palace—secretly, of course!"

"Wh-why...?"

"I don't know. I was simply told that a pizza should be brought and that nobody should find out. A carriage is waiting for you."

"Whoa..."

"Will you please come with me?"

Kaito nodded and hurried out of the shop. Parked in front of the mansion was a black-lacquered carriage he had never seen before. The paint looked glossy, and the decorations on the edges were in gold. It took no more than a look to know this carriage was in a completely different category from Lilia's cargo wagon.

The horse was an impressive specimen; it looked strong enough to get anywhere you might want to go in the blink of an eye. Standing by the horse was a man, dressed in black to match the carriage. On his head was a black hat, his nose and mouth were covered by a black cloth, and his eyes, which were just visible over his mask, glittered with intelligence. And was that a sword peeking out from under his black cape?

The man looked, overall, very dangerous. It was the first time Kaito had encountered such an intimidating person since arriving in this bucolic world, and he swallowed heavily.

"Are you Lord Kaito?" the messenger asked, his voice muffled by his mask.

"I am."

"The palace sent me. I have come on a secret mission."

"A secret mission...?" That sounded very serious, and Kaito's anxiety ratcheted up another notch.

"From what I have heard, you are the hero who brought the thing called pizza to this world of ours."

"I am..." Kaito nodded, thinking it didn't seem like that big a deal.

"The government is rather disturbed by the great and sudden revolution you've wrought."

"Uh...huh."

*Great and sudden revolution? It's just pizza.*

True, given what the elves had been eating before, it was probably quite a shock. But still...it was pizza.

"Hence, the conclusion has been reached that a quick and *quiet* investigation is necessary."

"Sure..."

*"Quiet"...* That was why they'd come in an ostentatious black carriage. People were already looking curiously from a distance.

*We totally stick out like a sore thumb.*

Edmond had once told Kaito not to expect too much of the country's soldiers, and if this was how an emissary from the palace acted, maybe that made sense.

A black carriage might have been a good idea if they had bothered to come at night. But showing up in the most visible place in town on a perfectly clear day? Kaito wanted to burst out laughing.

Suddenly catching himself on the verge of a titter, he had to give himself a quick pinch to hold it in. The messenger was the picture of seriousness, and Kaito suspected that exploding in laughter would be frowned upon.

"Well, then—" *Snort.*

Kaito desperately suppressed a guffaw.

"I understand. You just need me to make a pizza, right?"

"Yes. When you finish it, I will transport it and you to the castle posthaste."

"I'll get right on it."

The dough was already fermented, so all he had to do was shape it, put the toppings on, and bake it.

"Will just one be enough?"

"Yes."

"Uh, pizzas cost one silver coin each."

"You'll be paid at the palace."

"Got it!"

They were going to pay him. That meant this was real work. Kaito was excited.

*I think a tried-and-true margherita is the way to go.*

He quickly but carefully put the pie together, baked it, and put it on a tray with a silver lid.

"It's ready!"

"Please get in the carriage." The messenger held the door open for him.

The interior of the carriage was surprisingly cramped, but maybe that was just the way carriages were. His escort started the horse running.

As they came out onto the main street, Kaito heard someone call his name.

"Hmm?"

He looked out the window to see Lilia following them. She was pale-faced and running as fast as her legs would carry her.

"Don't run—it's dangerous! Stop that!"

He was in a carriage. There was no way she could catch up.

"Lord Kaitooooooo!"

Still, Lilia kept running. It was clear she was extremely worried.

"Huh?"

Strangely, the carriage was unable to lose her. Apparently, she was quite an athlete.

*She's fast!! Scary-fast!!*

Her furious pursuit made him think of the Noh play *Dojoji*. The girl Kiyohime, betrayed by the priest she loved, transforms into a giant snake and chases him down.

*Not that I've betrayed Lilia or whatever!*

The messenger seemed to sense something was wrong, because he picked up the pace.

"Hey!"

Lilia's legs finally gave out, and she tumbled spectacularly to the ground. Kaito could only watch as she pitched forward as if in slow motion, both hands outstretched to catch herself.

She slammed into the ground.

"Liliaaaaaaa!!"

People crowded around the collapsed elf girl, but the scene swiftly grew farther away.

*Oh, maybe she's okay.* But Kaito, unable to do anything for Lilia, found himself fretting as the carriage rocked along.

After a while, the palace came into view.

"Wow..."

The first things he saw were the towering spires. It was a textbook castle, done mainly in white.

*It looks like... Oh yeah.*

There was some castle in Germany that had supposedly been the model for Cinderella's Castle.

*Oh man, it's on the tip of my tongue.* Neuschbein *or something.*

While Kaito sat racking his memory, the carriage pulled up at the back gate.

The building was surrounded by a moat. At a signal from the driver, a gate opened slowly, and a heavy wooden bridge was lowered.

*Pretty sure I've seen this movie.* Kaito felt slightly impressed. *I'm in a fantasy world for sure...*

The carriage began making its way across the bridge. When it had entered the castle, the bridge gradually went back up.

Kaito's ride came to an end, at which point his escort reopened the door. "We've arrived, sir."

When Kaito climbed out of the carriage, he found himself in a dim, forested area.

"This way, please."

Shortly thereafter, they emerged from the silent woods and found themselves confronted with one wall of the royal palace. The messenger knocked several times on the wall, part of which proceeded to slowly retract. They were obviously going in the back door—or rather, the secret door.

"Now, inside. Quickly, please."

"Yes, sir!"

Kaito entered, his heart pounding. He was in a dark hallway. There weren't even any windows. Flickering candles on the wall provided the only illumination. Kaito followed the messenger until they arrived at a particular room. There were no windows there, either, leaving the place dark even in the middle of the day.

"Now, give me the pizza."

"Sure."

"Wait here, please." And with that, the messenger disappeared with the food.

The room was as bleak as a prison cell, but it had one table and one chair. Kaito, faced with few other options, sat down in the stiff seat.

*What's with the decor around here? This place is depressing.*

On the table sat a brass candelabra. The candle inside provided only the faintest illumination and wavered as if it might go out at any moment.

*I hope I get to go home soon...*

"Whew——"

Kaito breathed a deep sigh.

It seemed to be more than the guttering candle could take. The claustrophobic, windowless room was immediately thrown into darkness.

"Yaaaaaaaahh!"

*Oh crap!! I can't see anything!!*

Kaito groped his way over to the door and all but tumbled out into the hallway.

Fortunately, the door hadn't been locked.

"Geez, that scared me!" His heart was still pounding. *Being cooped up in that bizarre room in pitch-darkness is no joke!!*

"Now what...?"

Kaito stood in a daze in the dim hallway. There was no sign of another living soul.

*Should I wait for the messenger to come get me here? For how long?*

The candles in the candleholders on the wall flickered unsteadily.

*No good. If those went out, too, I think it would kill me.*

Kaito started down the hallway, looking for his escort. The path continued along a gentle curve, at the end of which he finally found a door. The door was ajar, light filtering out from inside. It looked like sunlight—pretty bright sunlight, at that—so the room beyond must have had actual windows.

Kaito peeked through the crack.

This room was the polar opposite of the jail cell–like place in which Kaito had been waiting before. The floor had a carpet of a deep-blue color, and all the furnishings looked gorgeous. This was a proper reception room.

In the middle of the room was an elf girl wearing a beautiful light-blue dress. Atop her halo of pale golden hair rested a striking crown. Even just standing there, the girl looked like she'd stepped out of a painting. Her beauty and style were flawless, and she oozed nobility.

"Wait... Could that be Queen Eleonora?" murmured Kaito.

Eleonora didn't move a muscle as she stared at the tray sitting on the marble table in front of her.

"Hey..."

*That's my pizza.*

Eleonora had her arms crossed and a suspicious look on her face, eyeing the pizza intently. Kaito remembered Edmond telling him that Eleonora was into healthy food and despised junk.

"...Hmph, so this is pizza."

She picked up a slice, her hand shaking.

"...Hrk."

Kaito's breath caught in his throat.

What would she do? Would she throw it away? The hero's heart raced as he watched her.

Slowly, almost fearfully, Eleonora brought the pizza to her mouth. She chewed thoughtfully—and then her blue eyes shot open.

*Maybe she doesn't like it...*

But the next second, Eleonora began digging into the slice with gusto. She looked like a starving animal tearing apart its kill.

"Whoa..."

No sooner had the queen wolfed down one piece than she started on the next, and soon, she had polished off the entire pie.

*Wait, wait, wait. That was an XXL. It was supposed to feed four people!*

And he'd thought Lilia had an appetite!

In his amazement, Kaito leaned a little too close.

"Oops!"

The door swung all the way open, throwing Kaito off-balance and sending him stumbling into the room.

*Crap!*

He looked up, and his gaze met that of the astonished Eleonora. Her light-blue eyes opened wide.

"Gyyyyyahhhhhhhhh!!"

She emitted a strange sound probably never before uttered by such royalty.

"Who in the hell are you?!"

Kaito couldn't help noticing the tomato sauce and cheese still clinging to her lips. The fingers pointed at him dripped grease.

"I-I'm very sorry! The candle went out, and— I mean, I thought no one was coming, so I went to find someone..." Kaito could hardly seem to get out a complete sentence. The queen was staring daggers at him. "You... You're Queen Eleonora, aren't you?" he asked nervously.

She nodded slowly. So this was the girl who'd had to assume leadership of her country at sixteen.

"...And I suppose you're the High-Calorie Hero."

"Yes, ma'am."

*No matter how many times I hear it, that still just doesn't sound cool...*

"So it was you who made this pizza."

"Yes, ma'am..."

Eleonora was gazing icily at him. "Belinda endorsed your pizza whole-heartedly, so I requested one to try for myself..."

"Oh, you know Miss Belinda...?"

His first delivery customer. A woman whose glasses made her look prudish but whose bookshelf full of Harlequin romances said otherwise. He'd heard she was employed as a tutor here.

Eleonora lifted her chin so she was looking down her nose at Kaito, her lips twisting into a frown.

"It is a vulgar food. Thick and oily, fluffy and rich—" *Drool.* The queen hurriedly wiped her mouth. "This is the first time I've eaten something so base!! You have some nerve bringing such coarse foodstuffs into my country!"

"I'm very sorry..."

"I simply cannot fathom why such an intelligent woman as Belinda would be so mad for such a thing. Though I will grant the flavor is very stimulating." Her eyes flitted to the empty dish. "I may need to consider imposing regulations on this food."

"......"

*Regulations? And just when I was about to expand the business...*

But he couldn't oppose the queen. Kaito tried desperately to think of a way to explain things to Eleonora, who was studying him gravely.

At the same time, a doubt began to creep into his mind. Eleonora had been acting very strangely ever since Kaito entered. What she was saying didn't match the behavior he'd witnessed. Could it be—could it be the queen had actually enjoyed the pizza but her pride was too great to let her admit it?

If so, he still had a chance. Kaito decided to commit to the possibility.

"Forgive me, my queen, for offering you something that does not please the royal palate! But you need not fear. I swear I shall never deliver a pizza here again, ever, for as long as I live!"

"You mustn't!!" Eleonora went pale. "You mustn't say that, because,

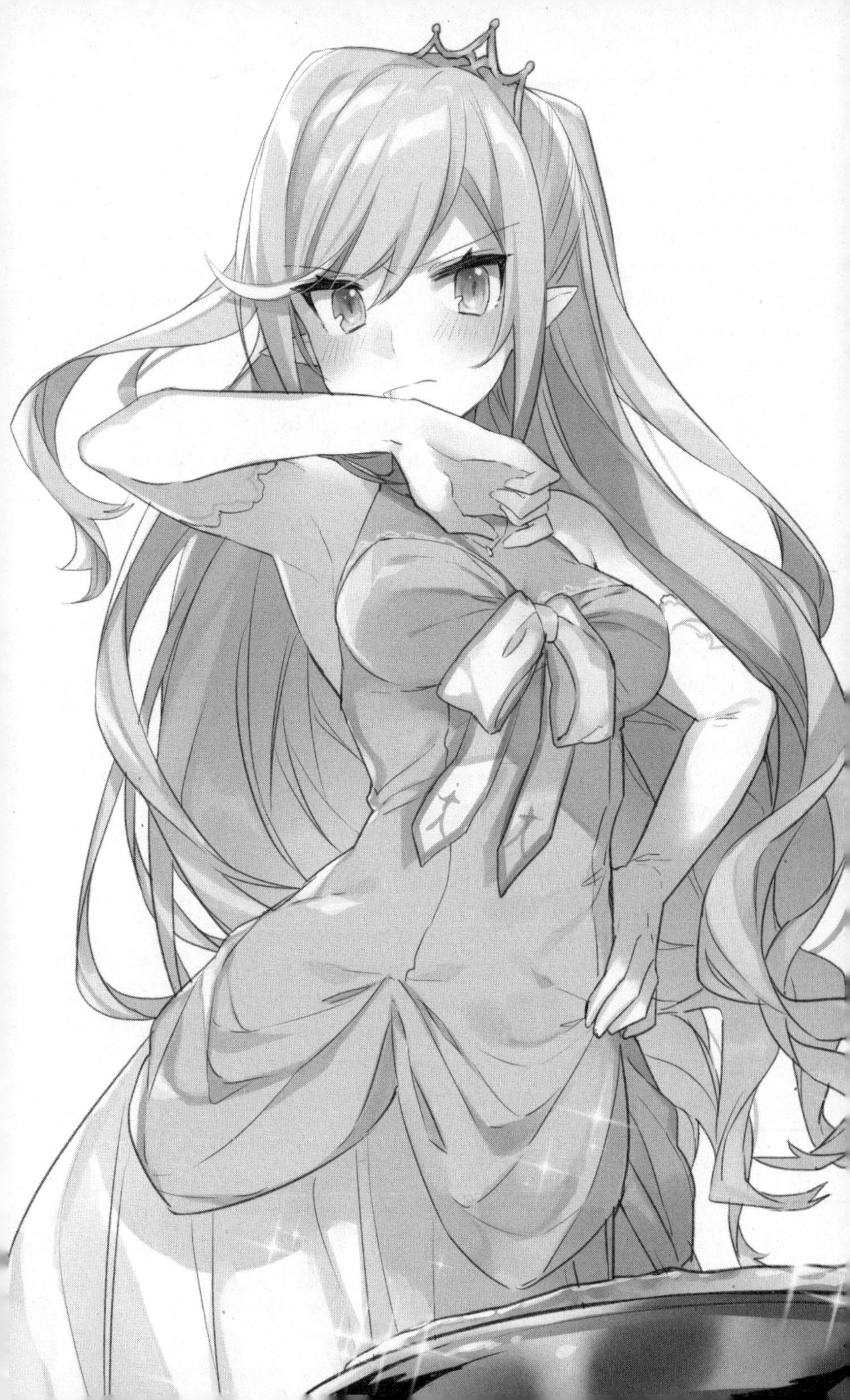

uh...um... Ah yes! This is the food the people are eating, is it not? The most popular menu item available? As ruler, it's my duty to understand what moves my subjects. My office demands that I eat pizza!"

"But regulations and sanctions could be most harmful to me."

Eleonora turned away from Kaito, seemingly in embarrassment.

"Ah yes, um. About that. I said that in the heat of the moment, or, well, what I meant was, perhaps in the worst-case scenario it might come to such things..."

"...I understand, Your Majesty." Kaito kept his head bowed in hopes Eleonora couldn't see the smirk stretching across his face. The quaking of his every limb was harder to hide, but oh well.

"For that reason—ahem—you shall bring me another pizza tomorrow." She was stealing little glances at Kaito to gauge his reaction.

"...Tomorrow, Your Majesty?"

"Yes. Research is required on my part to understand precisely what this 'pizza' is. Rulership can be a burden..."

"Indeed, Your Majesty." Kaito took care his voice didn't shake. What a contrary young woman. She obviously loved the pizza, but she refused to admit it.

"The carriage will be sent for you again. Come in the back gate, as you did today. I'll instruct the messenger what to do."

"Yes, ma'am!"

"Now take your payment and go home!! ...No, wait!!"

"Yes, Your Majesty?"

"This 'pizza,' as you call it, is that all your menu offers?"

Kaito suppressed another gale of laughter. *This queen is something else!!*

"No, Your Majesty. In addition to the margherita, we have a simple concoction of tomato sauce and garlic called pizza marinara and another called *capricciosa* that includes whatever ingredients you like."

"I... I see. Then for tomorrow, you shall bring two pizzas, one margherita and one marinara."

"Two pizzas, Your Majesty? Are you sure?"

"Why? Is it not feasible for you?"

"Quite feasible, Your Majesty."

*Surely she doesn't plan to eat them both herself? Although, given the way she inhaled that pie earlier...*

"How can someone so thin eat so much...?"

Eleonora was so thin and dainty that she looked like she'd break in half if you hugged her.

"Did you say something?"

"No, ma'am!!" Kaito quickly bowed and left the room.

He returned home the way he had arrived, in the carriage. As the vehicle bumped along, Kaito heaved a long sigh. That had been a close call, but all's well that ends well. What a relief to discover the queen liked his pizzas just fine.

When he got back to the headman's mansion, Lilia came rushing out. Her hands and face were covered in painful-looking scrapes.

"Lord Kaito!! Are you okay?! I was so worried!!"

"What about you? Are you in one piece?"

"I'm fine!!" Lilia smiled as if she'd won an award for bravery. The sight of her grin gave Kaito a rush of relief. "How did the pizza go over?"

"Well...I think we've got our first regular."

Kaito thought back on Eleonora cramming pizza into her face. He couldn't help but smile.

# CHAPTER 10

## Let's Go to the Great Market

The family was eating dinner when Edmond said with a smile, "Say, Kaito, tomorrow is the monthly Great Market."

"Oh, the one where people from all kinds of different countries show up?"

"The very same! The central square will be packed with shops—and people. There are always interesting things to see. Why don't you and Lilia go take a look?"

"Yeah, maybe..." Then an idea came to him. "Hey... Would it be possible to sell pizza there?"

"What?"

Hawking his food where there were lots of people around would get the word out, not to mention make him some money. Not bad, as sudden flashes of inspiration go.

"That sounds fantastic!"

"Yes, wonderful!"

Lilia and Fiona agreed with him.

"Do you have to apply for a vendor's permit or anything? I know this is really last-minute."

"You're supposed to apply prior to the market day, but you're our one and only hero—we'll make it work somehow!"

"Huh? No, please, you don't have to go out of your way..."

"There's a space set aside for our village; maybe you could use that. I'll go talk to the elf in charge of market affairs right away!" With that, he was up and out of the house.

"Is this really all right...?"

"It's just a bit of room to sell pizzas. It'll be fine. Oh, I'll help, of course."

"Thanks!"

It wasn't long before Edmond returned. "Everything is settled! We'll be selling vegetables. You can set up next to us."

"Thank you very much!"

Kaito's pizzas had proved to be well received, and he was even starting to save a little money from them. But it bothered him to have to rely on the headman's hospitality all the time. He had plans of building a two-story shop, with a pizza parlor below and a living space above. If possible, the restaurant would even have room for eat-in customers.

He'd asked the carpenter for a quote and discovered that he would need almost a thousand gold coins. Pizza netted him one silver coin at a time, and it took ten silver coins to make one gold coin. He had a long way to go.

*Welp, nothing to it but to do it.* Kaito was actually looking forward to the work of expanding his business bit by bit. The thought that he would get out of it what he put in inspired him.

"Okay, I'm gonna go get ready for tomorrow!"

\*

The next morning, Kaito put the pizzas he'd baked on trays, put the trays in a box, then climbed into the cart with Lilia. Edmond was driving.

"The weather is perfect! I bet the market will be busy today." Lilia looked happily up at the sky. Kaito watched, entranced, as the wind played with her gorgeous strawberry-blond hair.

*We're practically acting like husband and wife already. Going to the market together, selling pizza together... You know, this is pretty nice.*

The thought made him realize how comfortable he was in this place, how used to it he'd gotten.

"Oh, look! You can see it!" Lilia pointed into the distance, where a massive market had come into view. The place was packed with vendors' stalls, their colorful roofs competing for attention.

"Wow..." He had seen things like this before. It reminded him of local food festivals or amateur cook-offs, the sorts of events that were held in big parks or municipal facilities.

There were so many people crammed into the market that he could hardly imagine where they had all come from. All Kaito had seen since he'd arrived in this world was idyllic country scenery. He was almost overwhelmed.

"This way!"

Kaito shook himself out of his trance, jumped down from the cart, and followed Lilia and her family.

They waded into the crowd, where they eventually saw a group waving at them.

"That one with the green roof is for our village." There was a long table set up in the space, piled high with vegetables.

"Pardon me, but perhaps you could use that spot in the corner?"

"Sure! Thank you very much. I know my application was very last-minute."

"Not at all; it's our pleasure to have the Honored Hero here!"

"We're very grateful!!" The villagers' smiling welcome put Kaito's mind at ease.

He set his pizzas on the table. "So how does this work?"

"The signal to begin will soon be given, and then we all start selling at once."

"I see..." Now that he thought about it, Kaito realized that despite all the hustle and bustle, nobody was buying or selling anything. Everyone was setting up stalls.

Then a voice boomed through the area, so loud that the speaker must have been using some kind of amplifying device. "Welcome to the Great Market, everyone! Thank you all for coming, as always." The voice brought the chatter to an abrupt halt. "May our shoppers find great deals and our vendors great profits! Let the Great Market begin!"

A cheer rose from the assembled crowd in a wave. Suddenly, a mass of customers appeared, as if they'd been waiting somewhere.

"Fresh vegetables! Who wants fresh vegetables?"

"Buy in bulk and save!"

Beside Kaito, the villagers started shouting.

He took in a deep breath:

"Try the hero's own pizza! Limited to just thirty-two slices! Try some pizza; tell your friends!"

No sooner had he said this than people stopped to look. He didn't know whether they were responding to the unfamiliar word *pizza* or whether they were curious about this so-called hero, but either way, he'd succeeded in getting their attention.

"Pizza? What's pizza?"

"It's a food similar to bread. It's filling and invigorating!"

"All right, I'll take one slice."

"Here you go. That'll be two copper coins."

He was selling by the slice rather than by the pie, so the numbers involved sounded smaller, but perhaps thanks to the novelty of the food, Kaito found his stock selling quickly.

"Thank you very much!" He handed over a piece of pizza, along with one of the paper napkins he had brought.

The man now holding the slice looked like a foreign merchant.

"He's from the country along the coast," Lilia whispered. Maybe it was hot there, because he wore thin, loose clothing. In terms of his own world, Kaito might have considered it vaguely Turkish-looking.

Slowly and uncertainly, the man brought the slice of margherita to his mouth. The instant he did so, his expression changed.

"Incredible! What in the world is this? The cheese is so rich, and it melts together with the tomato sauce—and the crust is so fluffy!"

The crowd of passersby, who had all been watching the man intently, now showered Kaito with copper coins.

"One for me!"

"And me!"

"R-right away!" Kaito and Lilia handed out pizza as fast as they could. They had brought four entire pies, thirty-two slices in all, and they sold out in the blink of an eye.

"Amazing!"

"I've never had anything like it!"

Seeing the crowd of happy customers, Kaito relaxed. He was glad to learn that even people from other countries around here thought pizza was delicious.

"Give me some pizza, too!"

Customers continued flooding the stall well after Kaito had exhausted his inventory. He could only bow his head. "I'm extremely sorry, but I'm afraid we're sold out."

"Will you be here again next month?"

"Yes, I expect so..."

"Well, I hope you bring more than you did this time."

"I want to buy a whole pizza for myself!"

"I'll bring as much as I can!" Having somehow completely sold out of his stock, Kaito and company left the merchant area. "Phew..."

*I'm thrilled to get such a great reaction, but unfortunately, it doesn't look like I can meet the demand yet. Someday I want to get more helpers and make sure lots of people can try my pizza. Someday...*

"Nice work today, Lord Kaito!" Lilia was smiling.

"You, too, Lilia. Thanks." Kaito looked down at the sixty-four copper coins in his hands that he had earned from his pizza. "Hey, Lilia, what do you say we go shopping?"

"What? Really?!"

"There should be all kinds of ingredients here, right? I want to see what's what."

"Sounds perfect!"

"And..."

"Yes?"

"I'd like to get you a present. For helping me all the time. If you see something you like, just say the word. Er...we can't really spend more than we made today, though."

A smile bloomed on Lilia's face. Her cheeks turned the color of roses, and her eyes sparkled like emeralds. "A present from you, Lord Kaito? That would be wonderful!"

"Uh, I can't really, uh, get you anything expensive, but..."

"It's the thought that makes me so happy!" Lilia was off like a shot, hurrying down the street. "There's something that's always caught my eye..."

She stopped dead.

"Hmm?"

Lilia was staring transfixed at a display of fluffy cotton candy. It was light pink and quite cute.

*Drool.*

"Oh, is this what you want?"

"N-no!! Sorry, I just got distracted..."

The cotton candy was reasonably priced at just a single copper coin.

"Go ahead—pick one you like."

"Really...?"

"This store's only here once a month, right? I'll buy one for you."

"Th-thank you!" Lilia happily took a cotton candy.

"So which shop *were* you looking for?"

"This one!"

Lilia stopped in front of a stall selling cute knickknacks. Kaito couldn't help noticing that everything in the shop was food themed.

"Isn't this just adorable?" Lilia pointed to a hairpin with a strawberry-shaped decoration. It was only two copper coins—cheap. Kaito could easily buy it. He could have bought a bunch of them. Honestly, he would have liked her to choose something more expensive. But...

"Lilia... You know this isn't food, right?" he asked, just to be sure.

"Huh? Yes, I know that."

"So you're not gonna eat it or anything?"

"Of course not."

Kaito knew all about her appetite and wasn't completely sure he trusted her, but it was true that the hairpin would look nice on her.

"Okay. One of these, please." Then he gave the accessory to Lilia as a present.

"Thank you so much!" Her eyes welled with tears as she took the pin from him. Maybe it was the intense emotion that caused her pointy ears to bounce. "To receive a present from you is just so...!"

"Uh, it's—it's not that big a deal. Don't cry... Please?" People were starting to stare at the girl weeping in the street.

*They're gonna think I made her cry! I mean, I guess I did, but...*

"Here, why don't you try it on?"

"Okay!!"

The red strawberry hairpin went perfectly with her strawberry-blond hair.

"It looks great on you."

"Thank you!!" Lilia beamed happily.

*She's really cute...* Kaito was suddenly seized with the desire to pat Lilia on the head.

"Do you know where to get ingredients around here?"

"Yes, they're this way."

Lilia certainly seemed to know her way around, and Kaito followed her obediently. All around him, people were having fun looking at the various stalls. Everything imaginable was on sale. Dining utensils and clothes, knickknacks and accessories, along with items Kaito had never seen. It was no surprise that so many people showed up to shop.

Then he caught a whiff of a pleasant aroma that made his nose tingle.

"Wow..."

There was food all around him. Some stalls were cooking meat on sticks, while others offered sweet-looking candy.

*And I'm walking around with a young woman... It's like a date at a festival.*

"Looks like there's plenty of food stalls here."

But when he looked back, Kaito realized Lilia was gone; all he could see was a distressed old man looking at him imploringly.

"Please, Honored Hero, do something about your wife..."

"Huh?"

Lilia was crouched in front of the store, helping herself to the fruit on display.

*I guess she finally got too hungry to resist...*

"Lilia!!" His shout caused her to jump, but then she reached out for more fruit. "Stop!"

Lilia's hand finally froze, but her eyes continued to flit back and forth between Kaito and the food. He could see her weighing her desire to eat against her respect for him.

*Geez, she really is just like my dog back home... It would always check my mood while it was misbehaving.*

Lilia's hand started inching toward the fruit again.

"Lilia, leave it!" Kaito cried, unintentionally falling back on the same command he used to use with his dog. Lilia froze in place.

*Uh, I guess it worked.*

"Okay, stand up!"

Lilia stood bolt upright from her crouch.

"Now, come, Lilia!"

She obediently came over to Kaito.

"Good Lilia! Good!"

Kaito had mixed feelings as he delivered this praise.

*Am I on a date with a girl or a walk with the dog? Actually, isn't this exactly how my dog walks used to go? Better not think too hard about it...*

"I apologize. How much do I owe you?" He paid for the fruit Lilia had eaten.

"I'm really sorry... It just looked so good..."

"I know you were hungry. But tell me before you eat something, okay? I'll buy it for you."

"Okay. I'm sorry." She looked despondent.

"You really do get people from all over at this market, huh?" Many of the shoppers were elves, but their appearance and clothing were subtly different from those of Lilia and the other elves Kaito knew. Especially conspicuous were the elves with bluish-silver hair. They had beautiful light-blue locks and often wore clothes that exposed much of their skin. Maybe they came from somewhere hot. Both the men and women wore plenty of lovely accessories, making it obvious that wherever they came from was considerably more affluent than this country.

"Here, Lord Kaito, this area has unusual ingredients from all over the world."

"Oh, wow..."

Kaito let out a whistle of amazement.

The place was packed with all kinds of meat, fish, and vegetables. The unfamiliar seafood especially caught his eye. There were fish and shellfish the likes of which he had never seen before.

*Just one more reminder that I'm in another world...er, or maybe I just don't know that much about fish.*

At that moment, the crowd let out a collective gasp.

"What's going on?" Kaito stared at something that was being carried out by almost a dozen people. He could hardly believe what he was seeing. "Wait, that's—!"

"That's today's featured item. It's really rare, so there are lots of people here to see it." Lilia must have been used to it already, because she didn't seem very surprised.

What had so startled Kaito was a huge white squid, well over ten meters long.

"A g-giant squid...?"

"It's a kraken."

"A kraken!!"

The famous monster of the sea—just the sort of thing you might expect to find in a world with dragons.

Kaito looked, agog, at the kraken. Its white skin glistened just like a squid's. It must have been freshly caught, because its slimy tentacles were still twitching.

"It looks delicious..."

Kaito stopped, shocked to hear the words coming out of his own mouth. *I see a mythical monster like that, and the first thing I think about is eating it? But you* can *eat it, right?*

"Are krakens tasty?"

"It looks like something you could really savor, doesn't it?"

"Mmmm..." Kaito pictured skewers of rich squid meat, and his mouth began watering.

"But I've never eaten it myself... It's really expensive."

"Huh...?"

Someone who appeared to be a merchant was putting up a sign in front of the kraken. On it was written 1,000 GOLD PIECES.

"That *is* expensive!"

*That's the amount I want to raise to build my entire restaurant! So a kraken and a pizza shop cost the same amount... I would have liked to try that squid, but I guess that puts the kibosh on that idea.*

Kaito's shoulders slumped. "At that price, I guess they probably cut it up and sell it in pieces. Provided there aren't any *real* high rollers around..."

"True. And cooking something that big would be really tough."

Even a single tentacle, however, apparently commanded a price of ten gold pieces, well out of Kaito's price range. He looked down at his collection of copper coins, which had shrunk to about half its original size.

Suddenly, there was a hubbub behind him.

"What's going on?"

He turned and saw a young woman, one of the foreigners with bluish-silver hair, collapsed on the street.

"Are you okay?" Kaito asked, sprinting over and lifting the girl in his arms.

"Ergh..." She sounded sluggish but was still conscious. Her eyes fluttered open, revealing beautiful gold irises.

*Yow... She's gorgeous!*

No sooner had the thought crossed his mind than Kaito noticed how scant the girl's clothing was. Almost half of her generous chest was exposed, and he was all too aware of her body heat and the softness of her skin through her thin clothing.

Suddenly, he got the distinct feeling that someone wanted to kill him. He looked up to find Lilia staring daggers at him.

*What? It's not like I'm putting the moves on her!* Kaito felt as shaken as if he had been caught having an affair.

"I'll call a doctor right away!"

"No... I'm all right..."

"Sasha!" A huge man came running toward the silver-haired girl named Sasha.

"Father..."

"Are you okay?"

"Yes. I seem to have gotten a bit overwhelmed by the crowd..."

Sasha's father picked her up. "Thank you for helping my daughter. I want to express my gratitude. Will you come to my inn?"

"No, it's not—"

*—that big a deal*, he was about to say.

"I insist! It's not far from the market!" With that, Sasha's father set off walking. Kaito had no choice but to follow him, and Lilia, still pouting, trailed behind. This sudden invitation was a surprise, but Kaito was curious about the foreigners. Perhaps they could introduce him to ingredients with which he was not yet familiar!

They weren't far from the market when a huge three-story building came into view. Lilia gaped. "This is the nicest inn in our village!"

"Really?" Kaito noticed the carpet on the floor, and it certainly did look to be of high quality.

"Come on in; our room is on the third floor." Sasha's father showed them to a sprawling suite.

"This is incredible!!"

There was a reception area with a generous couch, and other rooms could be seen farther in. Between this and the expensive-looking clothes Sasha and her father were wearing, it was obvious they were rich.

Lilia was taking in the room, stunned. Sasha's father laid his daughter on a bed before returning to the reception area.

"A pleasure to meet you. I'm Aaron, a merchant from the nation by the sea."

"Oh, uh, the pleasure's all mine..."

Aaron had unusual ash-blond hair and the same golden eyes as Sasha. His skin had a light-brown color, perhaps from a tan, and he looked strong.

"Thank you for helping my daughter. She's a fragile thing... We came here hoping we might find some food that could give her a bit of vitality, but..."

"Oh, no, it was nothi—"

"I very much want to thank you." Aaron stared intently at Kaito. "Are you the hero everyone's talking about?"

"Huh? Oh, uh, yes, sir!" Kaito nodded, surprised.

"I knew the moment I saw you."

"You did?"

True, Kaito was the only one around here without pointy ears. Still, it surprised him to learn that word of the hero had spread to other countries.

"It's an honor to meet you. Rumor has it you make an unusual food-stuff. Pizza, I believe it's called?"

"That's right, sir. I would love for you to come and try some."

"Can it not be sent to other countries?"

"Right now, I've got my hands full just setting up shop. I do hope to make it more accessible one day, though."

*I could open a branch location in another country. That's not a bad idea... Not that I even really have my own place right now.*

"......"

Aaron studied Kaito with a sharp gaze. Kaito's heart pounded with the feeling that he was being appraised, like merchandise.

"Um..."

"Pardon me. I got lost in thought. First and foremost, I must thank you. Is there anything you want?"

"Oh, I couldn't. You don't need to repay me." Kaito didn't want to beg for money.

"I insist. Ask me for anything."

Kaito swallowed heavily.

*Well, there is... There is something I really, really want...*

"Uh...I'm interested in trying out kraken as an ingredient..."

"Are you, now?" Aaron raised an eyebrow, intrigued.

"Even just a tentacle would be enough. Is there any way you could help me get some? If you can, I'd like to use it to make a pizza to give to you and Sasha as a treat."

"!!"

Aaron's golden eyes went wide at this. "...You are a wiser man than I imagined."

"Um... Oh..."

"To take a gift, then make it even better and return it—truly superb."

"Th-thanks..."

*I think that's a compliment... Right?*

All he'd done was connect his desire to make a kraken pizza with Sasha's need for something that would give her a little energy.

"Very well! I shall do this for you. I have no small curiosity about this pizza of yours."

With those words, Aaron called someone in and said something to them.

∗

"Your kraken, as promised."

"Thank you very much!"

Aaron must have been a man with quite a bit of pull, because in no time at all, he had procured the kraken's tentacle. Of course, being from a kraken, it was almost a full meter long. More than enough for a pizza.

"Please take this as well."

"Wow! What's this?"

"Kraken ink."

"So krakens make ink, too..." Aaron gave Kaito a bag full of black squid ink. His surprise soon turned to delight, and he was sure it would make for a delicious pizza. "This is a big help! I'll go make the pizza—you just wait at your inn."

"I'll be looking forward to it."

After having the tentacle packed up, Kaito returned to his shop in high spirits.

"Okay! Time to show 'em what I can do!"

Once he had shaped the dough, Kaito mixed together some tomato sauce with the ink he'd been given. Almost immediately, the red of the tomato sauce vanished, turning black instead. A pinch of salt, and it was ready to go.

"Let's see here." An experimental taste revealed a rich umami that spread through his mouth. "Excellent!" The tomato helped neutralize any fishiness. This was going to be a good sauce.

*Drool.*

Kaito jerked upright at the unpleasant sound. Lilia was watching him, saliva beginning to creep out the edge of her mouth.

"Oh, sure. You can have a taste test." He put some of the sauce on a spoon and held it out to her.

*Munch!*

"Eek!"

Lilia bit down on the spoon with such enthusiasm that Kaito was afraid she might take his hand with it.

"Ahhh... It's delicious. There's a rough edge to the flavor that's unlike anything I've ever tasted..." Lilia was practically trembling with emotion.

"Yeah, you guys don't have any oceans around here, do you? Just hang tight for a while. *Leave it!*"

Lilia straightened up.

*Okay. Now I can concentrate.*

Kaito began chopping the glistening tentacle into thin pieces. He put the sauce on the pizza, then arranged the tentacle slices on top of it. The black sauce and white bits of tentacle looked rather plain, so he added dabs of tomato sauce here and there. He didn't put on any cheese, however, because he wanted to leave the focus on the main ingredients. Finally, he doused the whole thing in olive oil and baked it in the oven.

"All done!"

He put the pizza on a tray and covered it with a silver lid.

"I'll get the carriage!" Soon the two of them were hurrying back to the inn.

They knocked on the door of the third-floor suite, and Aaron soon appeared.

"We've brought the pizza!"

"We've been hoping you would. Sasha is able to sit up now, as well." When he ushered Kaito and Lilia into the reception room, they saw Sasha sitting in a chair. Her face was still pale, but she gave them a bow of her head.

"This is my seafood pizza—the Kraken Special!"

When Kaito set down the dish, Aaron and Sasha gave impressed sounds.

"Ho! So this is pizza!"

"Amazing... I've never seen a food like it before."

"So you've used the squid ink as part of the sauce?"

"Yes, sir. Please enjoy it while it's hot."

Aaron and Sasha both took slices, then Lilia and Kaito did, too. Kaito had prepared two pizzas to ensure there would be enough for four people.

"!!"

When Sasha took her first bite, her golden eyes went wide.

"This is *incredibly* delicious!! The umami of the kraken fills your mouth...yet it's so smooth and easy to eat!"

"That slight chewiness is perfect! The outside has a little snap, but the inside is soft. And the rich sauce goes perfectly with the simple, salty crust!!" Aaron, too, seemed genuinely impressed, his eyes shining.

"Ahhh... And it's not just the sauce—the thinly sliced kraken helps bring out the flavor..." A blissful expression appeared on Lilia's face.

The two pizzas vanished in no time at all.

"Now, that was a worthwhile purchase! What a surprise to see kraken prepared this way. You really put the flavors of your ingredients to best use!" Her father regarded Sasha excitedly. "And I've never seen my daughter eat so much at once!"

A healthy red glow had appeared on Sasha's pale cheeks. She no longer looked languid. She'd straightened up a bit, and there was a lively shine in her eyes.

"Man! I guess seafood pizza really does have special powers—I feel pretty energetic myself!" Kaito said. The whole idea of a seafood pizza was new for him, as he'd been using only vegetables and cheese.

"Thank you so much, Lord Kaito!" Sasha grasped Kaito's hand, leaving him flustered.

"Oh! Uh..."

Now that he'd gotten a good look at her, he could see Sasha really was a beautiful young woman. Her gold eyes had a bright gleam, and her striking ash-blond hair swayed gently.

"Oh, Lord Kaito, your collar..."

The collar of his shirt had folded over; she gently straightened it. Her hand brushed his neck, sending a shock through him.

*What the heck? This girl is surprisingly sexy...*

She was a little bit older than Lilia, he figured, but she exuded a calmness that made her seem very mature.

"I want to thank you. If there's anything I can do for you, please just tell me."

She came closer to him. She was slim, and her clothing left the cleavage of her generous breasts plainly visible.

"Er, ah..."

*This...this is bad! I feel like she's cast a spell on me! Like I could just fall into her arms!*

Kaito looked over at Lilia for help and found her wearing an angry expression like he had never seen from her before. She was squinting at them, and her green eyes were as fierce as a tiger's.

*Lilia's super-pissed.*

Those words floated up into Kaito's mind.

"Hrk..." He trembled before quickly regaining his sanity.

*Ohhhhh crap, is this scary! It's the quiet ones that are really scary when they're mad!!*

"Well then, uh, when you're feeling better, please come have some pizza at my shop. I want all kinds of people to be able to try it."

"We're here once a month for the market. I promise to come next month."

"We'll be looking forward to it." Kaito, feeling a rush of relief, was about to back away when Sasha suddenly pulled him close. She wrapped her arm around his neck in a hug.

"Lord Kaito, thank you so much!"

"Th-think nothing of it!"

*Yaaaaaaah, that chest! I can feel it! It's soooooo soft!! What the heeeeck?!*

Kaito successfully kept his thoughts from showing on his face, however, instead calmly extricating himself from Sasha's embrace.

*Geez! These foreign girls are passionate! That was so, so, so, so close!*

He thought he heard a strange sound next to him.

It turned out to be Lilia, grinding her teeth. She was looking at Sasha like a wild animal ready to do battle.

"Is your shop delivery only? Or is it a proper restaurant?"

"For now, it's delivery only, so I think it would be best if you waited until I had an actual pizza parlor set up." Kaito explained how he currently relied on the headman's good graces and how his shop didn't have anywhere for guests to sit down.

"So my first goal is to build a house of my own and a real pizza parlor. I expect I'll need about a thousand gold, so it's a ways off yet..."

Aaron was staring intently at Kaito. Suddenly, he slapped his knee. "Well, allow me to fund you, then."

"What...?!" Kaito looked at Aaron, unable to believe what he was hearing.

"Consider it an investment in the future. Perhaps when I come for pizza, you could make sure to prioritize my order. And when you expand into other countries, start with mine. How does that sound?"

"Ah..."

Even the simplest calculation put the value of this investment at nearly ten thousand pizzas. That was more than a lifetime supply. But Kaito was grateful for the offer.

"I can make a real pizza parlor with that money. It'll have space to eat in and everything. I hope you'll both come and visit!"

"I wouldn't miss it. I'll have the money sent to you later."

"Thank you very much."

"I look forward to seeing you again, Lord Kaito." Sasha slid up next to him and planted a soft kiss on his cheek.

"Whoawhoawhoawhoa!!" This sort of farewell was not customary where Kaito came from, and it left him reeling.

"Goodness, Lord Kaito!" Sasha giggled softly.

"Uh, well then, s-see you next month!" Kaito hurriedly left the room, trying to hide his beet-red face. "Phew..."

*I never imagined I'd not only get to make kraken pizza but even get an investor. This was one lucky day.*

Kaito started on the way home in extremely high spirits.

"Ahhh. Nice work today, Lilia," he said as they got back to the shop, but Lilia was sullen and silent. "Lilia?"

Lilia fixed Kaito with a piercing glare. "She was very pretty, wasn't she?"

"Huh?"

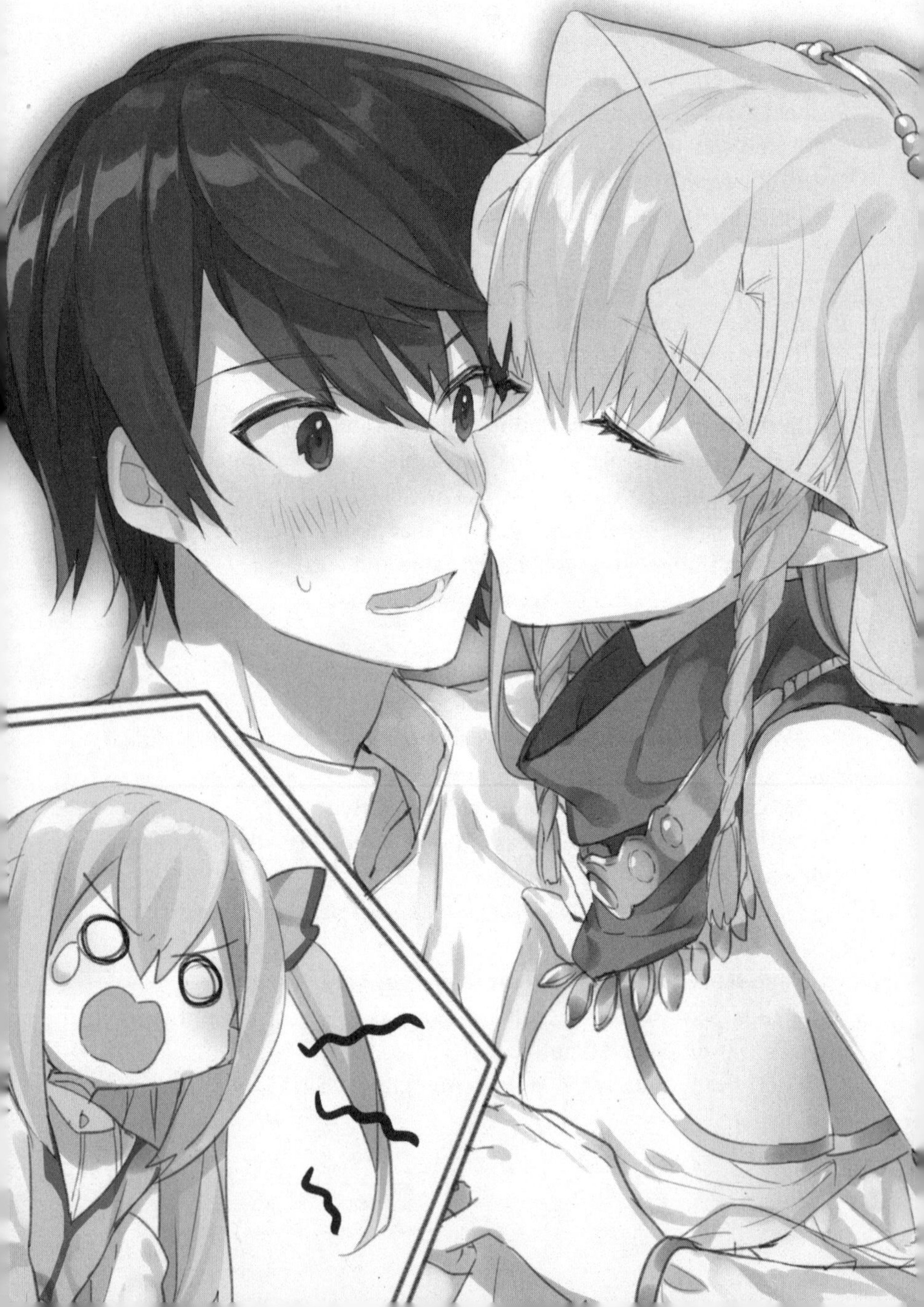

"Miss Sasha certainly has very big breasts and is very sexy. And her golden eyes looked like sunlight. That silver-blue hair is gorgeous, too."

"Yeah... She was something, wasn't she...?"

Sasha, the merchant's daughter, had a rich, full loveliness, something different from Eleonora's chilly beauty.

*Bonk.* Something hit Kaito in the head: a pizza peel. Lilia, holding on to the other end of the spatula, had tears in her eyes.

"Idiot!" She whacked him again. "Adulterer!"

"Hang on a second! Put that down!" He needed that for work! Lilia started beating him with her fists instead. She looked like a bantamweight, but she packed quite a punch.

"Yow! Ow, ow, ow! What do you mean, adulterer? What are you talking about?"

"Idiot! Idiot! Idiot! Stupid, stupid Lord Kaito!"

"Wh-what makes me an idiot? Lilia, would you please explain what's going on?!" He was completely baffled as to what had inspired Lilia to this random act of violence.

"You really are stupid, aren't you?! How can you force me to say it? To say that I'm jealous!"

"I think you've made yourself pretty clear! But what in the world are you jealous of?!"

"......!!"

Evidently, this was another misstep, because Lilia, her face still red, began pummeling him afresh. Kaito, still at a loss, tried desperately to ward off her blows.

"Stop, Lilia! *Leave it!*" The command had worked before, but now, Lilia's little fists kept raining down on him.

"Why won't you listen to me?! I said *leave it*, Lilia! *Leave i—!*"

Kaito had believed Lilia felt nothing more keenly than hunger, but he had a lot to learn about women.

Kaito took the money he'd gotten and immediately commissioned his new store. His dream of having a place to live and a pizza parlor all in one would finally come true.

*It's gonna be a while before the place is ready. Still, with a big new shop, I'd like to have a bigger menu, too.*

"I think I'd like to try out something new today!"

"Ooh, what is it? What is it?" Lilia's eyes sparkled. She was usually relaxed, but when the subject of food came up, she could suddenly be very energetic indeed.

"A dessert that goes well with pizza!"

Kaito had been thinking about it ever since Belinda had asked him for one. This morning, when he'd looked in his item bag, he'd found a new skill card. The name of a certain dessert had been written on it.

"A dessert... You mean like gelatin or pudding?" Lilia was perplexed.

"The High-Calorie Hero would never deign to make such low-calorie treats! He makes only the highest of high-calorie fare!!"

"Oh... Like... Like what?"

"Apple pie!"

Yes, the words that had been written on that skill card were *Apple Pie*.

It seemed the item bag would continue to replenish itself. Now that he was making lots of pizza and his level had gone up, he had been rewarded with more recipes.

*I wish that goddess would have told me about that. Figures I'd get stuck with the lazy deity...*

"So it's a dessert involving apples...?" Lilia asked.

"Exactly! I have the butter and the hard and soft flours to make the dough, but I'm missing the most important part—the apples!"

He had expected this day would come. At first, he had been given all the ingredients he needed, but now he would need to find some of them for himself.

*Guess that just means I managed to get past that very first stage.*

"Let's start by making the dough. It has to sit, so there's no harm in doing it now."

Kaito mixed the two kinds of flour he'd been given in a bowl and then added the butter. "Lilia, add a little water, please."

"Sure!"

Kaito continued mixing the batter with a spatula as Lilia poured in water bit by bit. He was surprised to find how much strength he needed.

"I guess making sweets is no walk in the park..." Kaito had only ever eaten premade apple pies, so he'd had no idea how much time and labor went into making one.

Once the dough had come together, he worked it into shape. Then he chilled it, and the piecrust, at least, was just about ready.

"Are there any apple orchards nearby?"

"There are! You remember my friend Elizabeth? Her house has an apple orchard."

"Perfect! How about we go for a wal— Eek!"

Startled, he realized the door had gently been pushed open, and Hans was staring at them through the crack. The light was reflecting off his blue eyes.

"Geez, Hans! Are you trying to do an impression of Jack Nicholson in *The Shining*?! You scared the crap out of me!"

"Apple pie... That does sound very delicious." Hans spoke in a low voice.

"You were *listening* to us?! Wait a second—why are you here anyway? Or are you just a stalker?!"

"I heard you had commissioned a new store, Honored Hero, and came to celebrate."

"I think you normally save the celebration for after it's actually built."

"Congratulations!" Hans held out a flower he appeared to have picked somewhere nearby.

"Uh, thanks..." Kaito took the flower as graciously as he could.

"I'd sure like to try some of that apple pie myself."

"I guess you can, but we're only just going to pick the apples. It'll be a while."

Kaito hoped that perhaps this implied that Hans could come back another time, but the woodcutter proved unable to take the hint.

"Oh! I'll help you!"

"Wha—?"

"You have to be pretty strong to pick apples. A fully loaded basket can weigh up to five kilograms."

"Is that so...?"

Now that he thought about it, Kaito realized he'd never been apple picking before. Maybe having someone with some experience along would be a good thing. It conveniently slipped Kaito's mind how much trouble Hans had gotten him in last time he'd shown up, and he found himself agreeing.

"Okay, then. Why don't you come along and help?"

"Gladly!" Hans's eyes were shining with happiness.

The three of them set off for the fruit orchard at the home of Lilia's friend Elizabeth. Naturally, they offered to pay for the fruit, and their price was eagerly accepted.

Kaito, Lilia, and Hans walked into the fields.

"Whoa..." It was apple trees as far as the eye could see. "This is incredible!"

"We do happen to be right in the middle of apple season," Lilia responded with a smile.

"So which ones are good?"

"If the bottom of the apple is either green or yellow, then it's good to eat." Lilia displayed a surprisingly robust knowledge of agriculture.

"Thanks for the tip! Well, let's get picking!" Kaito reached out for an apple, then suddenly stopped. "Uh, how exactly do you pick them?"

"Kind of...here. Grab it from the bottom, like this."

"Uh-huh, uh-huh."

"You twist it and pull up at the same time, and it pops right off."

"Let me try!" Kaito awkwardly grabbed an apple. "Let's see..."

He successfully separated the apple from the branch. "All right! A good start."

The three harvesters split up and began gathering apples. Just as Hans had warned him, Kaito found the unfamiliar work draining.

*It's tougher than I thought working with your hands over your head like this. Thank goodness there's three of us.*

His relief lasted for only a moment, though.

"Phew! How about we take a break?" Hans said as he took a jar of honey out of his bag. "Oops!" As Hans tried to open the lid, his hand slipped, and it looked like he was going to drop the jar. "Eeyi-yi-yi!" The rotund elf lost his balance—right next to their bushel of apples, as it happened.

"Han—" But before Kaito could so much as call his name, Hans took a huge fall into the basket.

*Squiiiiiishhh!*

"Haaaaaaaaaaaans!!"

There was a heartbreaking sound as their hard-won apples were destroyed, along with the basket.

"What the *heeeeeeeeeck*?!" Kaito, who realized he had been too cavalier about Hans's clumsiness, was aghast. "I mean, seriously! Aren't apples supposed to be tough? How do you squish an apple just by falling on it? What have you got in that stomach, a cannonball?!"

"I'm so very, very sorry!" Hans was shaking and covered in apple juice. Tears poured from his blue eyes. "How—how can I ever—? Oh! Only death can atone for—"

"Stop! You don't have to die because of some stupid apples!"

*Geez, this kid really looks like he's ready to do himself in! What do I do? Wait, I've got it!*

"Hans, I'm going to give you an important job to do." The woodcutter looked up, somewhat mollified by this. "I bet birds and animals are going to be very interested in our harvest. You have to guard it."

"Huh...?"

"This is a very important job, one I can only entrust to you. You want that apple pie, don't you?"

"I...I do!"

"Then get guarding!"

"Yes, sir!" Hans straightened up and began scanning the area intently. *Phew. That ought to keep him busy for a little while.*

"Okay! Back to picking!"

"I got us a new basket!"

"Nice work, Lilia! Let's see what the two of us can harvest!"

Kaito was starting to get the hang of apple picking, and it was going much more smoothly than earlier.

"Okay, I think this'll about do it. Twenty apples should be enough for today and tomor—"

He stopped in midsentence, his eyes bulging out of his head. The basket was empty.

"Whaaaaaa—? What's going on?" He didn't quite grasp the situation. "I'm sure I picked at least ten... Didn't I...?"

Then a familiar and deeply disturbing sound reached him.

*Munch, munch, munch, munch.*

Kaito looked at Lilia, whose back was to him.

"No way... Lilia?"

"Huh?" She jumped and turned around. There was an apple in her hand—and half of it was missing.

"What are you *doing*?!"

"I-I'm sorry!" *Munch, munch.*

"Stop it! Stop that! Lilia, *leave it!*"

"I'm sorry! I just got so hungry!"

"Ahhh, you could definitely starve doing this work!" Hans said as he downed an entire jar of honey as if it were a bottle of water with a *glug, glug, glug, glug.*

"......"

Kaito had clearly made some poor personnel decisions. A mega-klutz and a girl with a monster appetite—and these were the two people he chose to go apple picking with him?

*When will I ever learn...?* He clenched his fist with the shame of it.

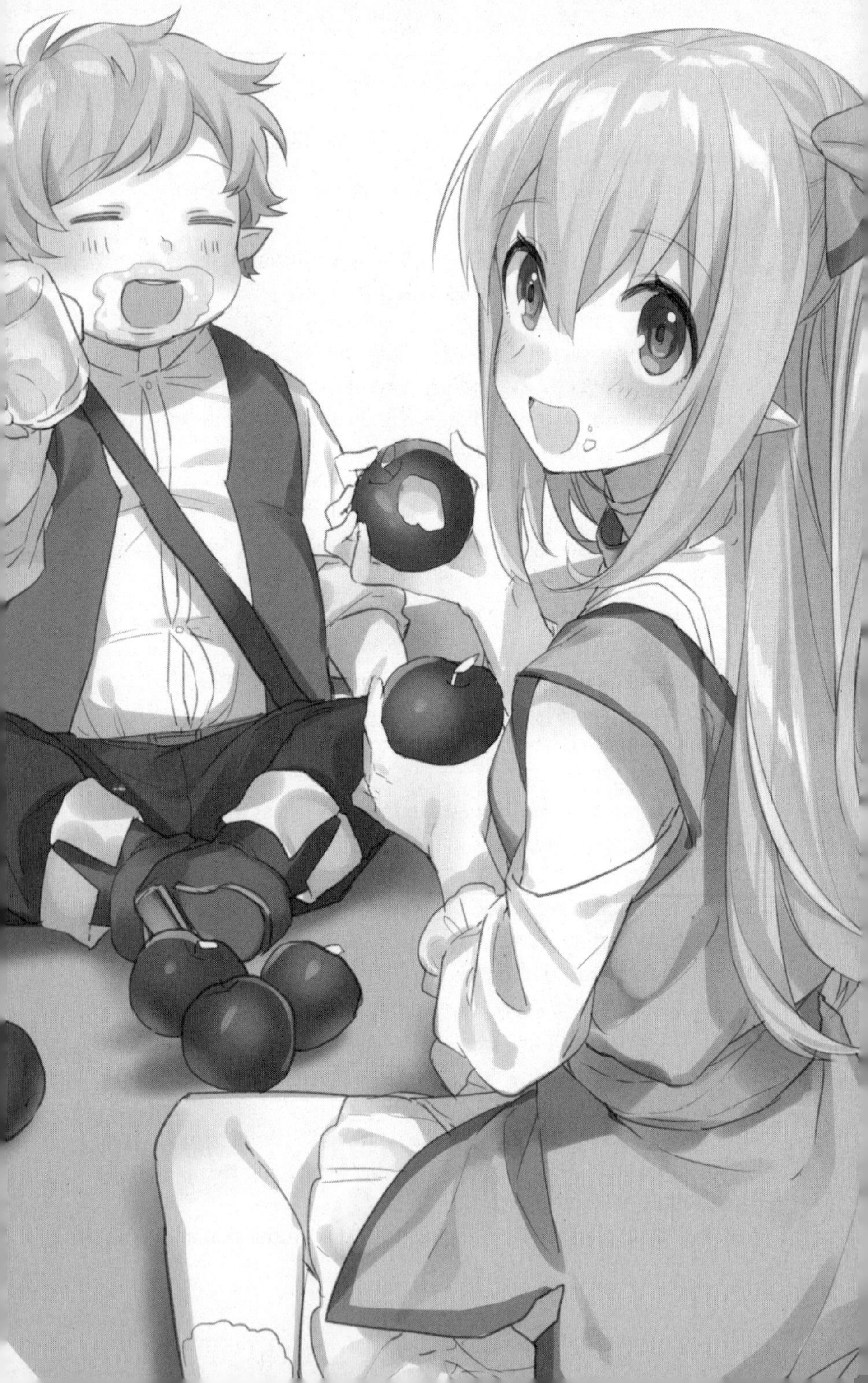

"I'm—I'm such a bad girl! I'm not worthy of you, Lord Kaito...!! Waaaaaahhh!!" Lilia dissolved into a crying mess right where she stood.

*Aaaargh! The trouble these people cause me...*

Cautiously, Kaito crept closer to Lilia, who had tossed herself on the ground, wailing.

*I just want to get my apples and go home.*

"Lilia, listen to me," Kaito said gently. Lilia looked up at him, her face drenched with tears.

"I want you to be the first person to taste the apple pie that I make. You understand that feeling?"

"Lord Kaito..." Lilia stopped crying and looked at him with moist, red eyes.

*Okay, I've got her attention.*

"So I do want you to be hungry, because it'll taste better that way, right?"

"Oh..." Lilia's eyes widened as she grasped what he was saying.

"So please...don't eat any more apples, okay?"

"...Yes, sir! I'll restrain myself!" She nodded firmly.

"Right, that's great. Maybe you could join Hans on guard duty?"

"Okay!" Fired up and overjoyed, Lilia went and stood next to Hans. The two monster eaters were keeping close watch.

"Phew..." Kaito was starting to feel pretty tired, but he couldn't stop now. He set out apple picking for the third time.

*Man, if I'd known this was gonna happen, I would have just come by myself to begin with... It would've been faster. Stupid, stupid, stupid me...*

Kaito heaped abuse on himself as he picked the fruit.

"I'm all done!"

Finally, he had an entire basketful.

At those words, Hans and Lilia came rushing over.

"I'll carry it for you!"

"No, I will!"

"No thanks, but I appreciate the gesture!" Kaito tried desperately to protect his basket from the two elves running at him with their arms outstretched.

*Don't crush or eat these apples I worked so hard to piiiiiick!! I can't pick any more! My muscles hurt and I can barely raise my arms and I'm covered in sweat and my feet ache and I just don't have the willpower or physical strength to do this all over again!*

"But—!"

"But—!"

His two helpers were still coming. *Sometimes the well-intentioned ones are the worst...*

"This is part of the hero's duty, too! Okay?" Kaito desperately invoked the one word sure to get their attention—*hero.*

"Oh, it is...?"

"Okay, then."

His ploy worked. Lilia and Hans stopped obediently where they were. Kaito resisted the urge to put a hand to his chest in relief.

✳

Once Kaito finally made it home with his apples, he went right to work. First, he had to peel the apple skins.

"Shall I help you...?" Lilia was looking closely at him. "I promise I won't eat any more."

"Well, all right then." Kaito decided to trust Lilia. He handed her an apple.

As each apple was peeled, he removed the core and sliced it. A certain crunchiness would enhance the experience, so he was careful not to make the slices too thin. Then he took a lemon he had gotten from Fiona and peeled that, too, before squeezing it over the apple slices, covering them in lemon juice.

"Oooooh!" Hans leaned in to watch as if this were deeply surprising.

"Hey, uh, Hans, don't get too close now, okay?"

Kaito added butter and sugar to the sliced apples and sautéed them.

"Wow... What a wonderful smell!!"

"Mm-hmm." Kaito greased a pie plate with butter, then dusted it with wheat flour. Next, he took out the dough he had set aside and cut it up, stretching and rounding each piece. He put the pieces onto the pie plate, then added the sautéed apples. He stretched the remaining dough and cut it into strips about a centimeter wide each. The piecrust was now in thin, rectangular strips, which he laid in a crosswise pattern on top of the filling.

"All right! Baking time!" He put the pie on a pizza peel, then into the oven. He kept a close eye on it and took it out just when it was perfectly browned.

"There! Done!"

The entire shop filled with the enticing aroma of apples and butter.

"Oooohhhh..." Lilia appeared absolutely entranced. Kaito cut the pie up, passing out slices to his companions.

"Here you go!"

"Bon appétit!"

It was his first apple pie—his first dessert. Excited but anxious, Kaito brought a piece to his mouth.

"Ow! Hot, hot, hot!"

The fresh-baked pie hadn't had time to cool. When he took a bite, though, the fragrant crust and the sweet juice of the apples filled his mouth.

"Wooow..."

The lovely scent of butter drifted to his nose. The sweetness of the fresh apples was thrown into sharp relief by the sour lemon juice.

"It's so sweeeeeet! And deliiiiiiicious!" Lilia's plate was already empty. "I've never had such a rich and satisfying sweet. Who knew fruit could be so powerful...?"

"There's seconds!"

"Yes please!" Hans shoved his plate in front of Lilia's. "I have a great idea!" he said, and he began dousing his new slice of apple pie in honey.

"Hans! Don't put honey on it!!"

*What, he wants it to be even sweeter?! And he's going to get even fatter!* Kaito managed not to say the words out loud.

"That's *deeeeeelicious*!" An expression of bliss came over Hans's face.

"Is... Is it?" Now Kaito was a little curious. "Maybe I'll try some." He dribbled just a little honey on his pie.

"Hey—that's pretty good!!" The honey deepened the sweetness even further and give it some punch. "Hmm, maybe I can invite people to add honey to taste!"

In any event, the apple pie was a delicious success.

"Looks like we've got ourselves a new menu item!"

*I'll have to let Belinda know.*

The three of them finished the pie in no time at all.

# The Vanishing Apple Pie

"All right! This is perfect!"

It was morning, and once again, Kaito had baked a whole apple pie. This way, he would be able to fill any unexpected orders, and if he didn't sell everything he had, well, he and Lilia and her family could share the leftovers.

Just then, Kaito heard a clatter from outside.

"Hmm?" He left the store and looked around but didn't see anyone. "Hans, is that you again?" Kaito walked to the garden. Hans's work as a woodcutter gave him a lot of flexibility, and he spent much of his free time stalking the High-Calorie Hero.

*It's nice to know he respects me, but it's a little creepy.*

Kaito would have to really give the elf a piece of his mind this time. He looked all over the expansive garden, but he didn't see anyone who looked like Hans.

"Huh? Could it have been my imagination...?"

Hans had a stoutness of stature quite uncharacteristic of an elf. It didn't make it easy for him to hide. If he'd been in the garden, Kaito would have found him. Even if Hans had tried concealing himself in the shadows, his belly would have stuck out and given him away.

Kaito went back to the shop.

"Wait a second... I know I left it right here..." He stared blankly at the table.

The apple pie he had just made was gone. He'd put it on the counter only moments before. Who might have come into the restaurant in the meantime? The only person he could think of was Lilia.

"I wonder if she knows anything about this... Oh, wait, that's right. Lilia isn't here today." It was the day for her sewing class, so she wouldn't be able to help out at the shop until she got back.

Kaito hadn't opened for business yet, so no one should have come in. And yet, like magic, the pie had disappeared.

"That couldn't have happened..."

How could there be a thief in such a peaceful village? Who was the criminal? What could they possibly want?

*Maybe they have something against me personally. Maybe they hate the High-Calorie Hero. Maybe they don't want me here. But who in this village feels that way...?*

It was a mystery! Kaito felt his excitement mounting.

Suddenly, a knock came at the door.

"Yes, come in."

Someone slipped into the store—it was Edmond. He was looking around anxiously.

"What's going on?"

The normally calm and collected headman seemed unusually edgy. "Oh, uh, nothing, I just—"

*Could he be the culprit? Maybe he's come to confess his crime. But why would Edmond steal an apple pie?*

"Edmond, I think you should just say exactly what's on your mind." This nearly caused the elf to jump. Then he surveyed the room for a moment. It was obvious he was hiding something.

"D-do you really?! But...but..." He looked like he was suffering.

"This is—"

*—really a lot of drama over one apple pie* was what Kaito was about to say. Before he could get the words out, though, the door of the shop flew open, and Fiona burst in.

"Pardon the interruption! *You!*" Her voice cracked like a whip. Edmond really did jump this time. "It's no use trying to run away! Now come here!"

"Ah, but, dear, you see, I was just... I was just talking to our son-in-law, Kaito, here and..."

"It's no use trying to talk your way out of this, either! The game is up! I know you were flirting with some cute young thing at the bar last night!"

"There's... Clearly, there's been some mistake. I certainly haven't been to the bar..."

"I have a witness. Come in here!"

At Fiona's command, Hans shuffled into the room.

"H-Hans!" Kaito and Edmond both exclaimed in unison.

"Now, Hans, tell them what you told me."

Tremblingly, the woodcutter opened his mouth. "Y-yes, madam. Last night, the headman took Miss Mona, one of the girls who works at the bar, by the hand and made her sit with him. Then he ordered beer and salad and thin-sliced ham! I'm *sure* you could've put honey on that!"

"Forget about the food!"

"Y-yes, madam!"

Fiona sounded much sterner than usual, and it gave Hans a start. The effect wasn't lost on Kaito and Edmond, either.

*I feel like she's even angry with me for some reason...*

Beside him, Edmond was as pale as if he had just been handed a death sentence.

"Then, he took Mona by the shoulders and tried to kiss her, but all he got was a slap."

Edmond gave a start and touched his cheek. There was no mark there, but it was as good as if he'd confessed.

Fiona's green eyes were absolutely on fire, as if anyone in her line of sight would be burned to a crisp.

*Geez! If looks could kill...* Even Kaito was frozen in place by her glare.

"*Dear*...I want to talk to you. Let's go back to the house."

"Yes, dear..." Edmond hung his head and followed Fiona like a criminal being led away by the police.

"Well done, Hans, thank you. Lord Kaito, you let him eat as much as he likes. Put it on Edmond's tab," instructed Fiona, and with that, the two of them were gone. Kaito's shoulders finally relaxed.

*Yeesh, talk about tension!*

Somehow, though, Kaito could hardly picture the serious Edmond trying to flirt. Then again, there was that advice the headman had given him that time Lilia's friends had come over. Something about laying a hand on your wife's friends being a one-way ticket to trouble.

*So...maybe he* was *speaking from experience...?* The idea made it a little easier to understand why Fiona was so upset.

"Phew! I was scared out of my wits!" Hans exhaled.

"Hans...don't you think that was a little harsh? Testifying against him like that?"

Kaito wasn't exactly trying to defend Edmond, but had there really been a need to squeal?

Hans hung his head. "I'm sorry... Miss Fiona told me I could have all the pizza I wanted, and I...I—"

"I know—there's nothing in the world that could outdo your appetite, huh?!" Kaito felt surprisingly sympathetic. Women knew how to manipulate people, and Fiona had found Hans's weak point. Anyway, Edmond had reaped what he'd sown; it was his own fault.

"So what do you want to eat?"

Hans's eyes sparkled. "First, I want to have some of your famous apple pie!"

"Uh...about that. I could have given you some right now, except..." He'd made that pie first thing in the morning for a situation exactly like this. What terrible timing.

"What's wrong?"

"It seems to have been stolen."

"Whaaat?! This is a disaster!" Hans began shaking.

"No, it's really not... You don't happen to know anything about it, do you?"

"I've been watching the entrance to the store all morning, but only you and Mr. Edmond ever went in."

This gave Kaito pause. "Wait... All morning? Why?"

"Oh, you know. I was just so hungry when I woke up. I've been waiting for the shop to open for an hour. Then Miss Fiona shouted for me..."

"...This stalker act is starting to creep me out..."

So maybe it really had been Hans who'd caused the noise outside.

Then he'd gone into the mansion when Fiona called him, explaining why Kaito hadn't seen him anywhere.

"What's a stalker? Is it a new menu item?!"

"Uh, no..."

Still, Hans had given him some valuable information. Kaito now knew no one had come in the shop in the last hour, ever since he'd baked the apple pie.

That meant the thief had to have sneaked in through a back entrance. Kaito turned around. He quickly opened the back door, letting out a sharp breath when he looked at the ground. There were pie crumbs all over!

"So they did come in through the back. I'm sorry, Hans. I'm going after the thief. Can you wait for a while?"

"Yes, sir!"

Close inspection revealed a trail of pie crumbs on the ground. Kaito followed it assiduously, exiting out the back door and going through the garden and then out onto the village street. He felt like Hansel. Or was that Gretel?

"So, what? The thief ate the pie as he went?" This didn't make much sense to Kaito. Why steal a pie and then try to eat it as you fled? Wouldn't it make more sense to go home first and then eat it? Why leave the proof just lying around? Kaito pondered all this as he followed the trail of crumbs. It took him all the way around the village, until he found himself at the front gate of the headman's mansion.

"What the heck?! Why did they come back where they started?" He just couldn't understand this criminal.

The trail led back into the garden, down a small path, and finally up to the servants' entrance of the mansion. Pie crumbs were still clearly visible. Kaito pushed the door open gently and entered the house. He found himself in a very large kitchen, but there didn't seem to be anyone there.

Kaito went out into the corridor. He could hear husband and wife arguing noisily in a room somewhere down the hall.

*I guess Edmond's not having a great day, either...*

Now Kaito was at the foot of the staircase. Apparently, the thief had gone up to the second floor.

"It can't be..." He followed the crumbs up the steps.

"But it is…"

The trail led right to the door of Lilia's room.

"I'm coming in," he said, and he opened the door. There was Lilia, just about to put the last bite of pie into her mouth. He had caught her completely and totally red-handed but found he just didn't feel like getting angry.

"L-Lorb Gaitob!!" She was trying to say *L-Lord Kaito!* but stuffed full of pie as she was, it was proving difficult. Crumbs sprayed from her mouth and scattered on the floor. Her pointy ears were quivering.

"I thought you were at sewing class?!"

"I-I'm very sorry! I stopped by the shop to say good-bye to you, and there was that fresh apple pie sitting right there, and it looked so delicious… And then, all of a sudden, I was walking away with it, and I kept wondering whether I should bring it back, and I kept nibbling on it as I kept wondering and walking around, and then I was back at home, and—and—there was just one bite left, so I thought I might as well finish it…"

"……"

*I always forget you're the queen of snacking…*

"I'm really, really sorry…"

"Yeah… It's…it's okay."

And so the mystery of the vanishing apple pie turned out not to be much of a mystery at all. Kaito was a little embarrassed at himself for having imagined he was playing detective.

# CHAPTER 14

# Eleonora, Revisited

"Phew..."

Kaito let out a gentle sigh. It had been a little while since he had last ridden in the elegant black carriage to the palace. Eleonora had been sending him orders every two or three days, but now it had been nearly five days with no word from her. He was starting to wonder if she had gotten tired of pizza, but then this morning, the messenger had suddenly appeared with that same striking black carriage as always.

"Are you here to order pizza?"

"No. To bring you to the palace."

"What?" Kaito had been entirely focused on the question of pizza, and this caught him off guard. What could be the matter?

The messenger was not the type to answer any questions no matter how persistently he was asked, so Kaito was left with no choice but to ride anxiously along in the shaking carriage. They went over the drawbridge and through the castle's back gate, Kaito entering via the secret door. Then he was once again spirited through the usual back room.

Eleonora was there. Her beautiful, slightly wavy platinum-blond hair reached below her waist, and she wore a small, elaborately worked golden crown. Her pale-blue dress followed the flowing lines of her willowy body; the cloth was embroidered but otherwise rather sheer. Her beauty and noble bearing, in Kaito's mind, approached the divine. He nearly found himself falling in love right then and there.

"It's been a while, Queen Eleonora."

Despite this entreaty, Eleonora only pouted, her brow furrowed in annoyance as she glared at him with eyes like ice.

*I wonder what's wrong. She looks really, really mad.*

The uncomfortable silence continued until Eleonora finally opened her mouth.

"...Kaito, don't you have something to say to me?"

"Huh?" he replied, taken aback. "And that something is...?"

Eleonora gritted her teeth at his response. "Playing dumb? You look so honest—I never took you for such a scoundrel."

"Huh??" Kaito didn't have the slightest idea what was going on. "I'm sorry, but I think maybe there's been some mistake..."

Eleonora gritted her teeth even harder. "There's been no mistake!"

"......"

He was at an utter loss as to what she was talking about.

*She doesn't order any pizza. Instead, she calls me to the castle. Why?*

Hesitantly, he asked, "Um, have I... Have I done something wrong...?"

This elicited a serious nod from Eleonora. "Indeed. That's why I've called you here. You still don't understand?"

"No, Your Majesty. Not in the slightest."

This seemed to be more than Eleonora could take. She stamped her foot. "Why, you—! Just how much further do you mean to humiliate me?!"

"Huh???"

Eleonora's pale complexion was turning redder and redder, the flush going right up to the tips of her pointy ears. She had crossed her arms and wouldn't look at him.

"The problem is...you know!"

"I do?"

*What do I know? What's the problem? This is getting more confusing by the minute.*

Eleonora was drumming her fingers nervously on one crossed arm.

*She looks a little bit like that goddess...*

"......"

"......"

The silence persisted until the queen couldn't stand it anymore, and she let out a scream.

"Just how dense are you, for goodness' sake?!"

"H-huh...?"

Eleonora shook her fist at him angrily, her platinum-blond hair quavering. Kaito could only stare in complete befuddlement.

*Wh-what the heck? She's lost it! There's no way I can deal with a hysterical ruler on my own. I wish someone would help!*

"Sh-shall I go call someone...?"

"You stupid, stupid idiot! Don't you dare call anyone! I chased everyone else out of here for a reason!" The queen's anger was burning so hot now that Kaito wouldn't have been surprised if she actually burst into flames. "Just how badly do you wish to disgrace me?!"

"D-disgrace you...?"

*When did we start using such fancy words like that? Wait, am I gonna be arrested for lèse-majesté and thrown in jail?*

Eleonora's face had grown as red as the apples Kaito used in his pies. He had to admit, the queen looked pretty cute when she was embarrassed—but he still didn't have any idea what was going on.

"...Argh! I see you're going to force me to say it myself!" She took a deep breath, steeled herself, and then finally blurted out, "I'm talking about—about this apple pie of yours or whatever it is!"

"My...apple pie?" He stared at her, still a touch perplexed, when a vase came flying at his head. "AAAAAHHH!!" He just managed to dodge the projectile, which smashed noisily against the wall.

"How can you make me spell out every detail?! Never have I been so humiliated!"

"Huh??" *Since when did apple pie become so embarrassing? What in the world is going on here?!* "P-please just stop throwing things at me!" Eleonora, having run out of handy missiles, had begun tearing the curtain off the window. "How is apple pie connected to any of this?!"

*And why are you so unhappy about it?!*

"How much more of a mockery do you intend to make of me?!" Eleonora erupted with rage. "Why was I not informed...?!"

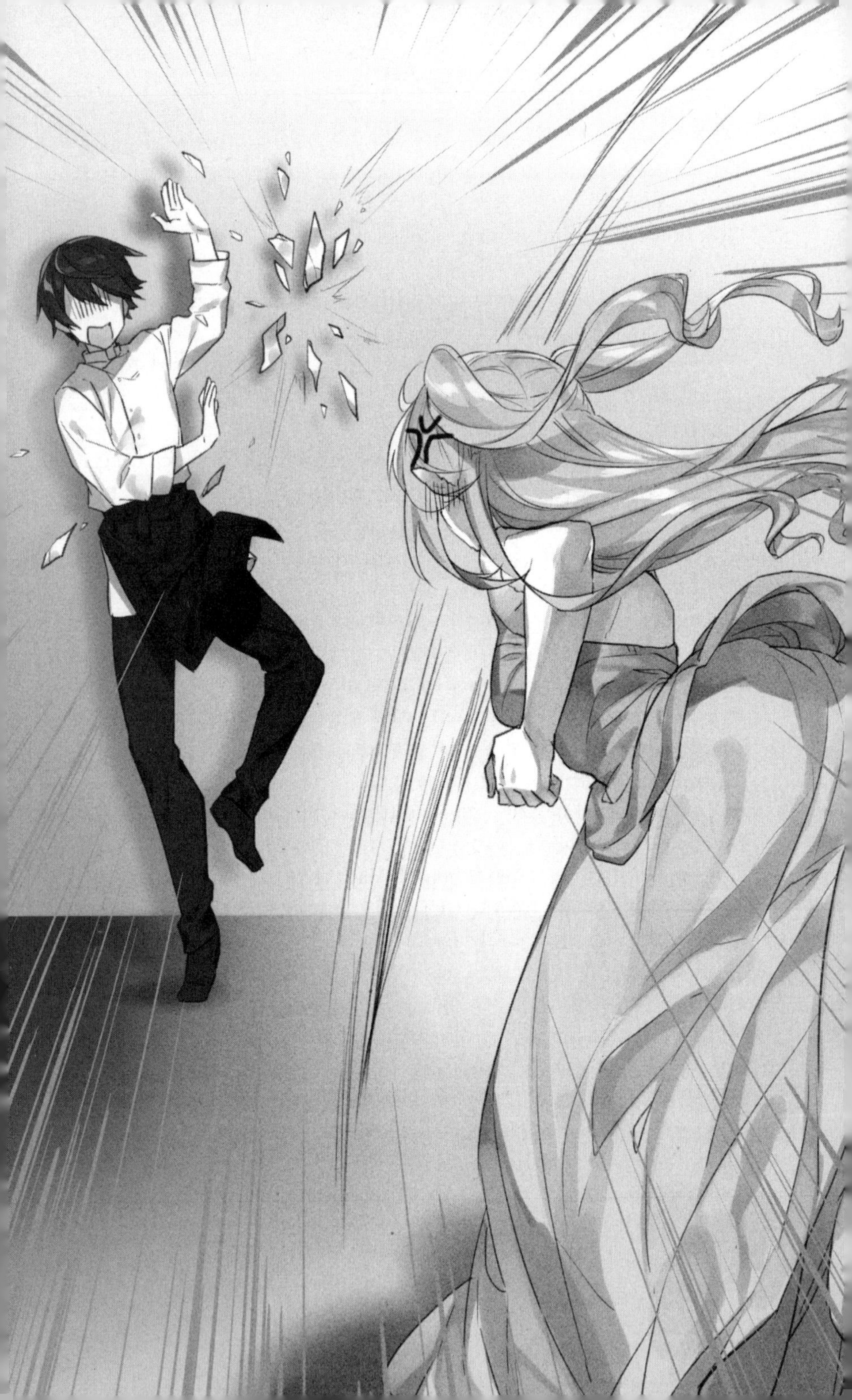

"Huh...?"

Kaito was bewildered. "You mean...about how I started making apple pies?"

"Yes!! Exactly!!"

"Huh? I mean..."

He had told Belinda, who had requested a dessert, right away and had delivered one to her first thing. So *that* was it. The queen must have heard about the apple pie from Belinda. There had been no orders from the castle lately, and so he had failed to mention the new menu item. Why couldn't the queen just say what she meant?

Cornered, Kaito suggested, "P-perhaps you'd like to...try it...?"

"Ahem. Well, if you insist on receiving the royal opinion on your foodstuffs, I suppose I have no choice! Bring me one immediately!" She sniffed and looked away.

"I'm sorry, but...I can't."

The queen did a double take. "What?! Are you saying you won't let me have one?!" she howled.

"I've already sold out for the day..."

Apple pie had turned out to be a big hit, and he had run through the day's supply with his advance orders.

Disappointment was plain on Eleonora's face. Her eyes were moist, as if she might burst into tears at any moment.

"What I can do is bring you one fresh from the oven tomorrow morning, okay?"

Instantly, Eleonora's face shone. She quickly put on a more somber expression and cleared her throat pointedly.

"Erm, a queen can hardly refuse to entertain a heartfelt offering from one of her subjects."

"Very heartfelt, Your Majesty." Kaito had to pinch himself to suppress a smile.

*She just can't say what she wants... But making food for people this eager to eat it—that's what it's all about.*

"And, er, what time will you be bringing this offering?" Eleonora asked, glancing at Kaito, who replied with a smile:

"I'll be here first thing in the morning."

# The Bonus-Item Mission

"Bonus item...?"

Kaito studied the card he had taken out of his item pouch. It had become a habit to check the bag each morning, and this morning, it had yielded this unfamiliar card.

"What's that?" Lilia asked innocently.

Kaito casually flipped the card over, then stared, agog, at the word on the back.

"C-c-c-cola?!"

"'Cola'?" Lilia didn't understand.

"*Cola*... No way—really?"

He had assumed that sweet nectar would never pass his lips again after arriving here. That most beautiful of beverages, cola...

"Why do you look so surprised?"

"Huh? Because..."

The elves drank mostly water and tea. Fruit juice was about the only sweet drink around. To think he might have a taste of cola, that beautiful and terrible thing...

Kaito swallowed heavily. It would be all right for him. He was used to it. It might prove too stimulating for the elves, though. Maybe he should keep this one to himself...

"Lord Kaito, are you all right?"

"Fine! Just fine!" He chased the wicked thought away. "How about we clear this mission and get us some cola?!"

The objective written on the card said *Use ingredients from this world to make a delicious pizza!*

"......"

Had he earned this card by making the kraken pizza? That had used only ingredients from this world. Now, though, it looked like he would have to come up with something new.

"'Ingredients you can find only in this world...'" The image of a dragon flashed through his mind. That would certainly be something unique to use in his pizza. However, he didn't even know if dragons were edible, and he didn't think he would have much luck defeating a monster that even the royal soldiers couldn't overcome.

*How about we try something a little easier?*

The elves' country was rich with agriculture. Surely there was something there he could use.

"Lilia, what kind of ingredients might work in a pizza?"

"...Tomatoes?"

"Okay, but we're already using those. We need something new!"

"...Apples?"

"Right, which are in our apple pies. You know what? Never mind." Lilia was clearly not going to be any help here. Kaito resolved to go find some ingredients himself.

*I should be honest here. I just* really *want to drink some dang cola!*

*I want to drink that delicious tongue-tingling, amber-colored carbonation!! I want to hear that* fizzzzzz *sound it makes!!*

*All right, let's do this!!*

*

Kaito took Lilia out ingredient hunting. There were plenty of different crops growing in the fields.

"Lilia, what's that?"

"That's cabbage."

"Lilia, what's that?"

"Potatoes."

*Darn. All totally normal stuff. I knew whatever just happened to be growing nearby wouldn't be good enough.*

Then Kaito spotted a plant with strange leaves growing by the roadside.

*These leaves...they look a bit like a carrot. Suppose there's a vegetable growing underneath?*

"Lilia, what's this?"

"That's a mandrake." She uttered the terrifying name nonchalantly.

"M-m-mandrake?"

The terrifying plant of legend? The one that screeched when you pulled it up, heralding your death? That certainly counted as an ingredient he would find only in this world. But...

"How do you harvest it?"

"You don't. But it's supposed to taste bad anyway," Lilia said, once again, casually.

"Really? Someone's eaten it?"

"Hans accidentally picked one a while ago. It turned into a lot of trouble."

"Hans did?!" Then Kaito gulped. "By l-lot of trouble, d-do you mean...?" Could Hans's persistent idiocy be a legacy of his encounter with the mandrake?!

"The mandrake's scream startled him so much that he fell in the river and got swept away."

"Oh, you mean that kind of problem." Kaito relaxed. That didn't sound so bad.

"They're unusual enough that we decided to try to eat it, but no matter how much we cooked or boiled it, it was always hard and never tasted good. That's why nobody picks them."

"I see." So mandrakes weren't actually that dangerous, but they weren't that tasty, either. Oh well.

Kaito looked around. The village might not have been the best place to search for rare ingredients.

"Can we head for the forest for a while?"

"Sure," Lilia nodded, still unconcerned. Kaito took that as a sign that the woods weren't too dangerous.

Kaito, a city boy through and through, wasn't very handy when it came to the natural world, so it was with some hesitation that he ventured into the forest.

"Lilia, you're sure you know the route?"

"It's not a problem in this part of the woods. But if you want to go very far in, you'd need a professional guide and some preparations."

"Uh, we'll just stick to what's right here!"

The woods were bright with midday light, and with Lilia, who knew the area, at his side, Kaito walked among the trees without much trepidation. Unfortunately, though, he found only ordinary trees and grasses. Nothing that looked especially edible.

*I was hoping for some berries or mushrooms or something.*

Just then, he heard the flutter of large wings above him. There was a creaking sound, and the light wavered. Kaito looked up in amazement at a bird flying directly overhead. Its wingspan must have been at least two meters.

"Wh-what the heck is that?"

"It's very unusual. That's a thunderbird."

"A thunderbird?"

"Uh-huh."

"What? I thought thunderbirds were bigger than that."

"That's about as large as the ones around here get. They vary by area."

"So they really are rare, huh?"

"Around here they are. Normally, they live deeper in the woods."

Kaito looked up at a nearby tree. He guessed it was at least a meter in diameter. The leaves and branches made it hard to get a good look, but he thought he saw some kind of nest.

"Hey, is that...a thunderbird nest?"

"Looks like it."

"And do they lay eggs?"

"Probably."

A light bulb went on over Kaito's head.

*Thunderbird-egg pizza! That's the ticket! That just screams "alternate world," doesn't it?!*

Kaito didn't have any confidence in his ability to hunt an actual thunderbird, but getting some eggs would be just a matter of picking them up, right?

*Then it's mission clear, and that cola's all mine.*

"You know how to climb trees, Lilia?"

"Not very well. And I'm not dressed for it..."

"Ah..."

Lilia was wearing a skirt that went down to her knees, but her legs and feet were bare.

"Okay, I've got it! I'll go up there!"

"Will you be all right?"

"...I don't know!!"

When it came to climbing trees, Kaito had a very vague memory of having tried it back around the time he'd been in elementary school. Or maybe he hadn't. Either way, he had to get up that tree, or he would never get his eggs.

Kaito placed one hand firmly on the trunk and reached out for the nearest branch. Then he felt his outstretched hand and his foot begin sliding.

"Erk..."

He slipped straight back down the trunk, landing on his butt on the ground.

"Awww..."

Darn! He couldn't even climb one little tree. He came to his knees, disappointed.

"Lord Kaito, are you okay?"

"I thought I'd finally found a rare ingredient..."

"Do you really want eggs that badly?"

"Not just eggs. Thunderbird eggs! A delicious ingredient that can only be found in this world! That bird looks too strong for me to catch, but I thought maybe I could at least get an egg..."

"Would the bird itself be good enough?"

"Sure. Thunderbird pizza sounds pretty good, right?"

"Wait here a moment." Lilia went running back the way they'd come. Kaito sighed and leaned against the tree.

*It seemed like a good idea at the time...*

When Lilia came back a few minutes later, she was carrying a wooden bow and arrows.

"Huh?"

"I'll get it when it comes back to its nest."

"Huh? Huh?"

Unlike Kaito, who was starting to quake visibly, Lilia was very calm as they waited for the thunderbird. At length, they heard the flapping of huge wings and a screeching cry.

Lilia quietly readied an arrow and took aim at the thunderbird, its wings spread wide. Kaito held his breath. Lilia looked like the bravest person in the world to him at that moment.

Then she let the arrow go.

"GRAAAAAAHHH!!"

With a tremendous cry, the thunderbird came crashing down. The arrow had pierced it clean through the throat.

"Whaaaaaaaat?!" Kaito looked at the thunderbird lying in front of him, dumbfounded. How could it be so easy? "Lilia, that was amazing!"

"It was? But all elves can use bows."

"Really? So archery is an elf's specialty…"

But it was still pretty amazing.

The two of them carried the thunderbird home. Lilia took care of the rest. Watching her, Kaito felt like he was watching someone wring the neck of a chicken. She pulled out all the feathers and drained the blood. Maybe he would have felt squeamish before, but now he was too excited to taste the meat to be frightened.

"Here you go!"

Kaito took the thunderbird meat Lilia had given him and sliced it into manageable pieces. He boiled it up, then worked in olive oil, parjee, hanahakka, and salt. He got the crust ready and covered it in tomato sauce. Then, on went the Thunderbird slices, along with some mushrooms to give it some texture, followed by cheese sprinkled over everything.

A dash of olive oil, and into the oven it went.

"Here it is—my Thunderbird Special!"

He and Lilia each took a slice.

"Bon appétit!"

The flavor of the aromatic meat filled their mouths.

"Oh yeah, it's good!!"

"Wow, I never knew thunderbird was so delicious!"

"It's got a crisp, simple taste like chicken tenderloin, but it's definitely meatier. You can feel the weight of it!"

He'd never expected the pizza to come out so well. The meat was soft, the flavors complemented each other perfectly, and there was no unpleasant aroma.

"Phewww..." In no time at all, the two of them had finished the dish.

That was when it happened. There was something like a flash of light, and a bottle of cola appeared on the countertop.

"Yeeeeeeeessssss, colllllaaaaaaaaaa!!!" Kaito grabbed the bottle and broke into a dance.

"Lord Kaito, are you okay?"

"Thank you, Lilia! This is all thanks to you!" He took out two glasses and poured the cola into them. "Taste this! I want to share it with you."

"So this is cola... It has a nice amber color, doesn't it?" Lilia eyed the bubbly liquid with interest. "Is this alcohol?"

"No, just a carbonated drink, but it's pretty stimulating. Don't let it take you by surprise."

With some hesitation, Lilia brought the glass to her lips and drank a few experimental sips.

"!!"

With a look of shock, she put it back down.

"Wh-what is this?! It's so tingly! And sweet and delicious! I've never drunk anything like it before!"

"Right? Ahhh, cola's the best..." Kaito gulped down the rest of his drink and exhaled in satisfaction. "That feels so good."

This was a day that would be long remembered for the meeting of gourmet dishes from two different worlds: thunderbird-meat pizza and cola.

*A toast to a mysterious and wonderful combination.*

Kaito and Lilia smiled at each other, then clinked their glasses.

The construction of Kaito's restaurant was coming along nicely. When it was ready, he planned to move out of his current location—which, granted, was only just next door. But there was one thing that weighed on him.

"Hmm..."

Specifically, the fact that this would mean leaving the home of the headman, whose hospitality he had been enjoying ever since he arrived. When that happened, there would be the question of what to do about Lilia. For some reason, it seemed he and Lilia were betrothed.

*What will I do when I build a new place to live?*

Should he bring Lilia with him? But that would be as good as declaring they were going to get married. Recently, they had been going everywhere together, and it was true he enjoyed it and felt quite comfortable with her.

*But am I really ready to get married? Hmm... I kind of am, but then again, I'm kind of not...?*

"Lord Kaito!" Suddenly, Lilia came flying into the pizza parlor, startling Kaito out of his ruminations.

"Y-y-yes?"

"Hans has been hurt!"

"Wha—?!"

*What, did he fall down again? He's such a klutz.*

"He went into the forest to cut wood and ran into a dragon!"

"Wait, what?!"

✳

Kaito and Lilia baked one of Hans's beloved apple pies, then went over to the woodcutter's house.

"Hans, are you all right?!"

When they opened the door, however, there was Hans, looking the same as always.

"Honored Hero!" he exclaimed, jumping up from the sofa. Kaito had thought Hans might be bedridden, but he seemed every bit as energetic as usual. There were some scratches on his face and hands, but not much more.

"So, uh...I heard you ran into a dragon."

"Ooh, what have you got in your basket?"

"N-nothing important. What about that dragon?"

"What'd you bring?" Hans's eyes were fixed on the basket. The way they were glowing was a little bit scary.

"Are you hurt, or—?"

"What's in there?" Hans wouldn't let it go. The basket was the only thing he was interested in.

*This isn't getting us anywhere.*

"...We brought you an apple pie to help you recover!"

*Drool.*

"...Yeah, yeah. I know. I guess we'd better start by eating it."

Kaito sliced up the pie and put it on some plates, and Hans begin pouring honey on it with gusto.

"Ha-ha-ha! Delicious, delicious... Sweet, rich apples and crunchy pie..."

"Well, I'm glad you like it, anyway." Kaito waited patiently for Hans to finish, the woodcutter's mouth messy with honey.

"Ahhh... Now, that was good!"

"So anyway, Hans. Tell me about what happened when you met this dragon."

"Of course! I went into the forest as usual to cut some wood."

"Like, deep into the forest?"

"No, not far."

So about the same place where Kaito and Lilia had found the thunderbird. Surprisingly close to town, then.

"Then suddenly, I heard an earth-shaking *thuuuuuud*, and there was a dragon next to me!"

"......"

"Gosh, dragons sure are big, aren't they?! I panicked."

"Makes sense." If Kaito had run into a bear in the woods, he would have panicked. And a dragon was considerably more threatening than a bear.

"I wanted to run away, but my feet were frozen. I decided to roll away instead, but there was a slope, and I slid down it..."

"Ah, so that's how you got hurt?"

"Yes. But thankfully, the village wasn't far from where I stopped rolling, and I was able to escape."

"I'm glad to hear it..." Hans seemed to have the worst luck. "So what happens now that a dragon has been sighted near the village?"

"Hmmmmmm. Well, for starters, everyone will be on the alert, carrying their pots."

"Pots?"

"You strike it with a solid object, and it makes a noise. They say dragons hate that."

"So, bear bells, basically...? Does that really work on dragons?"

"No idea!"

"Uh...huh."

It was just as Kaito had thought: These people had no real plan for dealing with the dragon. If it would just go back home to the mountains, that would be all well and good, but if it decided to pay the village a visit instead, there would be trouble.

"Okay. I'll talk to Queen Eleonora and see if I can get her to lend us some soldiers."

"Soldiers?"

"From Queen Eleonora?!" Hans and Lilia looked at Kaito in astonishment.

"Right. I want the military here to protect us on the off chance that the dragon comes to the village and starts attacking people."

"Sure, but the soldiers of our country aren't very strong!"

"Right! I don't think they would be much help!"

Hans's and Lilia's pronouncements were not very heartening.

"Well, uh, okay. But I still think it's got to be better than nothing. Lilia, can you take me to the castle in our cart?"

"……"

The two of them departed Hans's house; Lilia walked along silently.

"Lilia? Is something wrong?"

"…You said you were going to Queen Eleonora."

"Huh? Sure. She's the big kahuna around here, right? It's the quickest way to get what we want."

"You know I can use a bow!!"

"Whoa, whoa. I'm not going to make you—or let you—do anything that dangerous. Let's leave this to the professionals, all right?" Even if it sounded like they might not be very good professionals.

"Are you sure you don't really just want to see Queen Eleonora?"

"Hmm? Did you say something?"

"Nothing!"

Lilia brought out the cart, pouting all the while. When they explained what was happening to the guard at the castle gate, he let them right in. Okay, so maybe security wasn't the tightest around here.

When they were brought to Eleonora's room, they found Belinda with her.

"Miss Belinda, I haven't seen you for a while."

"Goodness, Lord Kaito. Fancy meeting you here. Is something the matter?" Behind Belinda, Eleonora was desperately pressing a finger to her lips in a shushing motion. There seemed to be something she wanted to keep secret, but what could it…? *Oh.*

"Are you here to deliver a pizza? …What am I saying? Of course you're not. Queen Eleonora hasn't shown any interest in pizza."

"Huh?"

Kaito looked at Eleonora in surprise. She was pressing the finger to her lips harder than ever now; it looked like she might start hissing *Sssssshhh!* at any minute.

*No way. Has she actually been pretending to Belinda that she doesn't like pizza? What an obnoxious queen!*

"You're right. I'm certainly not here to deliver a pizza."

This at last brought a look of relief to Eleonora's face.

"A dragon has appeared near the village, and I'm here to request soldiers to help us."

"I see... So it's that time, is it...?" Neither she nor Eleonora seemed very surprised. They looked almost as if they were used to this.

"What should we do, Belinda?"

"Well, let's see. I suppose we should keep an eye on the situation. Let's start by sending two soldiers. Dispatching too many at once would only upset people."

"All right. I'll have two soldiers head over. If they travel by horse, they should be there soon."

"Thank you very much!"

*I knew talking to the queen would be the quickest way....*

Deeply relieved, Kaito returned to the back gate.

"Huh?"

When he arrived, though, he looked around in confusion at finding Lilia and the cart gone.

"What...what happened to Lilia?"

He tried asking the guard, but the man only got a distressed look on his face.

"Er, she said she was going ahead back because she had something to do. I'm afraid we don't have a carriage ready for you, Lord Kaito..."

"......"

Kaito had a bad feeling about this.

"I'm sorry—please take me to the village! Hurry!"

Rattling along in the black carriage, Kaito was beside himself. The moment he got back to the mansion, he searched all around the house.

"Liliaaaaaaaaa!!"

But she wasn't in her room. Kaito dashed back downstairs and into the kitchen.

"Lord Kaito, what in the world is wrong?" asked a surprised Fiona, who was doing some cooking.

"Um, you don't happen to know where Lilia is, do you?"

"Lilia? She went out earlier. She had her bow with her."

"What...?"

*Her bow?!*

He thought back to what she had said not long ago.

——*You know I can use a bow!!*——

*No...*

"Lilia!!"

Kaito raced back out of the house. If Lilia was planning to slay the dragon or drive it away, she would have headed for the forest. Kaito ran down the path to the woods at breakneck pace.

"Liliaaaaaaaaaaaaaaaa!!" He shouted at the top of his lungs as he went, until he began hacking and coughing. His throat was dry, he had trouble breathing, and his heart felt like it might give out at any time. Finally, he came to a stop.

"Oh..."

When he looked around, Kaito realized he was smack in the middle of the forest. Without Lilia and her knowledge of the area. Without even a weapon.

"Oh, no, no, no, no, no."

Was this a double misfortune? *Am I in more trouble than Lilia now?*

All was quiet in the woods, and sunlight streamed through the trees pleasantly. But a dragon could show up anytime. Fear set Kaito's heart racing.

That was when he heard a rustling in the underbrush.

"Eeeek!!"

When he turned to look, though, Lilia was standing there, bow in hand.

"L-Lilia!!"

"Lord Kaito, what are you doing h—? Oops."

When Lilia let her concentration lapse, her hand slipped off her bowstring, and her arrow went flying.

"AAAAHHHHH!" The arrow grazed Kaito's cheek as it rocketed by before burying itself with a *thud* in a nearby tree.

"Lord Kaito! I'm so sorry!" Lilia rushed over to Kaito, who had fallen down from the shock. "I'm so sorry! I should have paid more attention!"

"Oh, you..."

Kaito gently reached out to Lilia. His hand brushed her smooth, pale cheek.

*She's unbelievably dense and clumsy and stupid, and I can't take my eyes off her for a second. But she means an awful lot to me. So much that I ran straight into a dragon-infested forest without so much as a weapon just to help her.*

Kaito finally recognized his own feelings.

"So it's *me* who's the bigger idiot..." The thought brought a smile to his face.

"Lord Kaito?" Lilia was looking at him, worried.

"Lilia, I know it's a ways off, but eventually, I'm going to have my own pizza parlor."

"...I know."

"Will you run it with me?"

"What...?" Lilia's green eyes went wide, then filled with tears. "Are you saying...?"

"Yeah. I want to marry you."

Lilia was shaking, overcome with emotion. "That makes me so happy..."

"I'll work hard to get those flowers I'm supposed to give you. Bluebells and whitebells, right?"

"Yes..." Lilia nodded through her tears.

"So, listen... Don't do anything this crazy ever again, okay?"

"All right." Lilia smiled.

"How about we go home? If we actually find that dragon, it won't be pretty."

At just that moment, though, screams and the sound of people beating metal pots came from the direction of the village. Kaito and Lilia looked at each other, then rushed off toward their home.

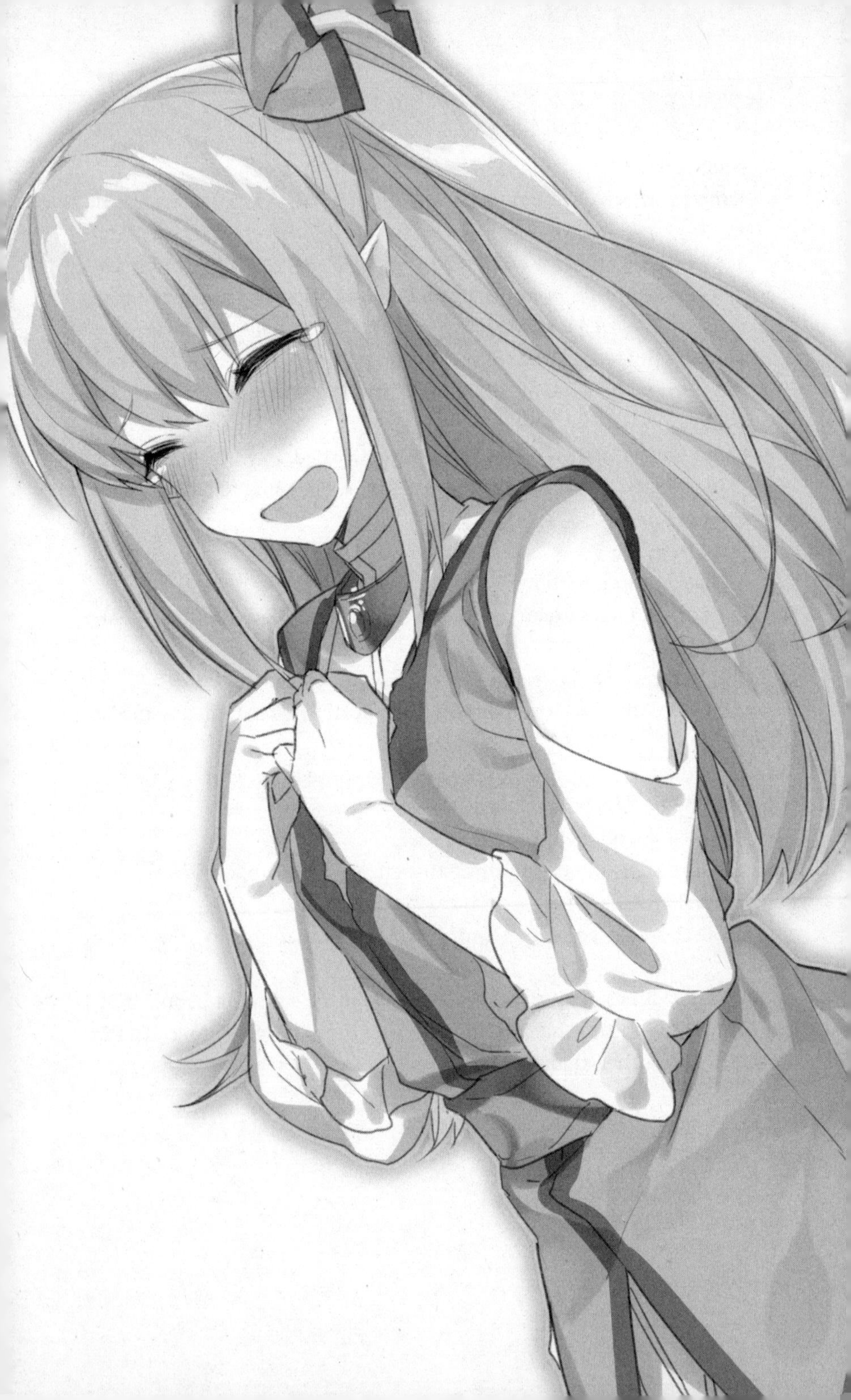

# CHAPTER 17

# Showdown with the Dragon

When they got out of the forest and back to the village, they found people fleeing in every direction.

"What's going on?!"

"The dragon has come to the village!!"

"!!"

Things couldn't be worse.

"Where are the soldiers from the palace?"

"They went to Hans's house!"

"Why there?"

Kaito couldn't understand. Was the dragon after the woodcutter?

"Whatever. I'm going to go help him. Lilia, you get back to the mansion and evacuate with your family!"

"No!" Lilia said firmly. "I'm your wife, Lord Kaito, and I'm going to stay at your side and protect you!" The conviction in her voice made her seem awfully brave and dependable.

*She's not wrong, though. She does know how to use a bow, and that makes her a lot tougher than the "High-Calorie Hero."*

"All right! Let's go save Hans!"

Kaito and Lilia threaded their way through the panicked crowd.

"Oh!"

They could see the huge dragon in the distance. The tallest buildings in the village were just two or three stories, so the monster was easily visible. He was a classic dragon, covered in dark-green scales, and he was standing right in front of Hans's house.

"Hans—please, please be all right!"

Kaito could see two people who looked like soldiers facing the creature down with their spears.

"Wh-where's Hans?!"

"Inside!"

"Can you handle the dragon?"

"No, sir! We were just asked to keep watch! We don't have anything but our spears and our swords!"

Well, that didn't inspire much confidence. But it was true; those spears didn't look like much to kill a dragon with.

"Can you at least chase him away?"

"We've been beating everything metal we could get our hands on ever since he arrived, but it doesn't seem to bother him at all!"

That was when Kaito registered that the villagers who had assembled to help Hans were carrying pots and kettles.

"What is the dragon doing?"

"We don't know, sir. He's just staring at the house..."

Then Hans stuck his head out the window.

"Lord Kaito!"

"Hans!"

*What to do, what to do?*

Kaito wasn't having any flashes of inspiration. The panic seemed to be all he could focus on.

At that moment, the dragon noticed the open window and brought his head very, very close to it.

"AAAAAAAAHHHHHHHHH!!" Hans tumbled backward.

"Hans!"

But the woodcutter did something entirely unexpected: He took one of his omnipresent jars of honey and flung it straight at the dragon's face.

"Oh!"

The jar connected with the monster's snout and then bounced into the front yard.

"Stop!" one of the soldiers called, his face pale. "Don't antagonize him!"

Slowly, ploddingly, the dragon began moving. It brought its face down to the jar of honey in the yard. The jar had broken open, and the honey had poured out. Now the creature began slurping it up.

*Grrrrrrrrrrrummmmmblle.*

A great noise could be heard from the dragon's stomach.

"Huh?"

Now that he took a closer look, Kaito could see how thin the dragon was. The poor creature was all skin and bones. "Is he...just hungry?"

Could the dragon have chased Hans through the woods, all the way to his house, just because he wanted some of that honey?

"Hans, wait right there!"

Kaito dashed off to his pizza parlor as fast as he could, Lilia close behind him. He burst in the door and pulled out some dough.

"Lilia, shape this, quick!"

"Right!"

The elf girl had been by Kaito's side throughout his career, and she worked the dough now as if she had been doing it her entire life. Kaito put toppings on the prepared crust at top speed.

"Done!"

Kaito baked the pizza, dropped it on a tray, and rushed back to Hans's house. The dragon was still lapping up the honey in the yard.

Kaito swallowed heavily. He was making a dangerous gamble.

*But I'm the High-Calorie Hero! And this is how I'm going to save Hans!*

He crept closer to the dragon. Everyone watching him gulped.

Kaito delicately set the plate down next to the creature. The food gave off a wonderful aroma. The dragon turned toward it with intense interest.

"Whoa!!"

"Lord Kaito!" Lilia grabbed him protectively.

"Lilia! It's too dangerous—stay back!"

*Sniff, sniff, sniff, sniff.*

The dragon was smelling the pizza intently. It looked like he was being cautious; he had never seen this food before. But then his appetite won out, and he gulped the pizza down in a single bite.

"!!"

Immediately, the dragon's tail went up. His scales, which had been a drab green color, grew brighter before their eyes, regaining their richness and luster.

"You want some more?"

Maybe the dragon could understand human speech, because he nodded eagerly.

"Then wait right there!!"

*

After the dragon had eaten no fewer than twenty pizzas as fast as Kaito could make them, he closed his eyes in contentment. His once gaunt stomach was now bulging.

"If you get hungry again, feel free to come back any time."

The dragon looked at Kaito with boundless gratitude. Then he gave one great flap of his wings and flew off toward the mountain.

"Phew..." Kaito breathed. At the same time, a raucous cheer went up.

"Huh?!"

The villagers came up to him one after another, smiling broadly.

"Lord Kaito!"

"That was brilliant! That's our hero for you!"

"You sent the dragon on his way, and no one was so much as hurt!"

"Thank you so much!"

Kaito wasn't quite sure what to do, surrounded by the grateful populace.

"Lorb... Lorb Gaitooo!" Hans came pushing through the crowd, his face tear-streaked and his nose snotty. "Dank you sooo buuuchhh!" There was a rather unpleasant squelching sound as the woodsman embraced the chef. Hans buried his face in Kaito's shoulder, smearing the young man with tears and snot.

*Uh...I guess I can always have my clothes washed when I get home.*

"I'm so glad you're safe, Hans!"

He patted the woodsman on the back. Perhaps Hans found this reassuring, because he began weeping in earnest.

"Ha... Ha-ha-ha-ha-ha-ha!" Kaito, however, found himself laughing as he rubbed Hans's back.

*I really was kinda a hero there!*

When he'd arrived in this world, he had never imagined he might find such satisfaction here. He smiled at Lilia, who had worked her way up next to him.

"That was wonderful, Kaito!"

"Queen Eleonora!"

He turned as he heard someone behind him call his name. He found the queen accompanied by a battalion of soldiers.

"Wh-what are you doing here...?"

"I got a little worried. I came here to back you up, but I see you handled everything yourself!"

"Well, thank you."

"Indeed. A true hero... You might even be fit to be my husband, perhaps."

"I'm sorry? Come again? I didn't quite catch that last part."

"Er, it's nothing. Just thinking about the future."

"?"

"Anyway, bravo, High-Calorie Hero!"

This elicited fresh excitement from the villagers, who broke into applause.

"Whoa!!"

The next morning as he was heading for the pizza shop, Kaito was startled to find the dragon sitting outside the door.

"Wh-what's up? Hungry again?"

The dragon dropped the shining golden sword it had been holding in its mouth square at Kaito's feet.

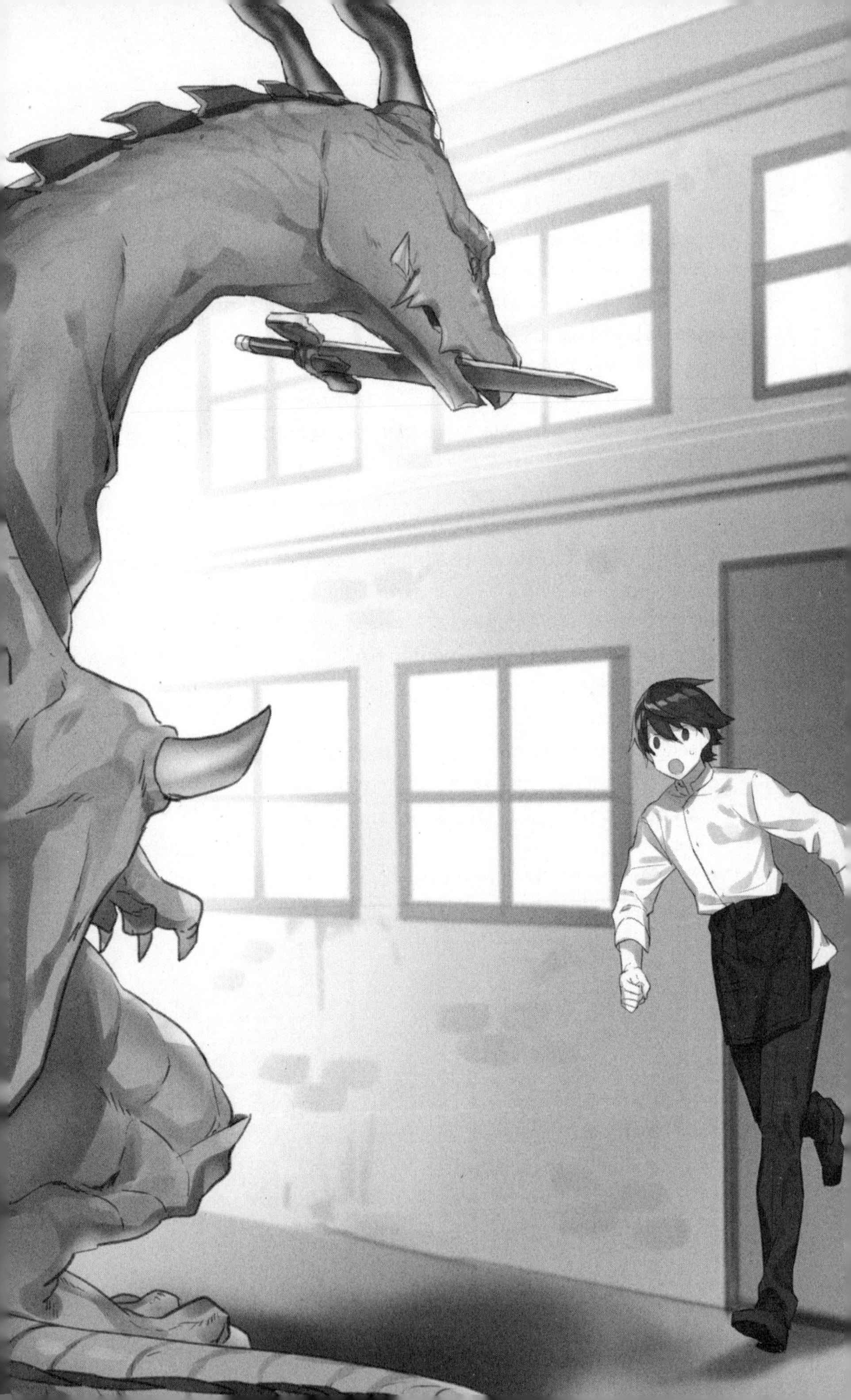

"Huh? What's this? Are you...paying me?"

The dragon nodded.

"Yeah, okay. Hold on. I'll get cooking right away."

He hung out the shop's sign. It was going to be another busy day for this alternate-world hero and his pizza parlor.

# Afterword

This is my first alternate-world story. Some of you are probably wondering why I decided to write about pizza. There's no big secret, but let me make a few notes about how this story started.

I was in a certain café discussing what my next book might be about, and I decided to write a sort of slice-of-life story set in an alternate world. Slice of life, a picture of a nice, slow existence... It has a good ring to it. I love it. I was feeling very tired, and I thought I would enjoy writing something like that.

Since I was going to go to all the trouble of writing this story, I thought about writing about a business, and that's how this all started.

"I'll bet it would be fun to run a restaurant..."

I love delicious things.

"This imprint has a lot of male readers, so it would be good if the restaurant served something men like. Let's see... There's ramen, *yakiniku*, sushi, beef bowl, curry, hamburgers..."

I listed off all the foods I could think of that guys might like, but none of them quite fit. I really need a "key word" I connect with in order to start writing.

Just at that moment, I remembered a conversation I'd had with a particular male acquaintance. He had told me how, in high school, he used to cut class to stay home and make pizza.

"Why'd you do that?"

"I don't remember… I wonder why…"

So I never really got closure on that anecdote, but the high-schooler/pizza connection stayed with me.

"Pizza… How about pizza?"

Pizza is kind of in vogue, and it seemed like you could tell a lot of different stories about it. Above all, it sounded like something that would be fun to write about. And as far as foods guys like to eat—well, everyone loves a good pizza!

I got the okay from my editor and started writing the book you now hold in your hands.

It was determined that the book would be a series of short stories, so I thought it would be nice if I could do it like one of those overseas dramas or sitcoms. Each of the chapters has a beginning, middle, and end of its own for you to enjoy, but a greater flow runs through the book, and everything wraps up nicely at the end. Personally, I think I did a pretty good job achieving that, but what do you think?

Comedies are a lot of fun whether you're writing or reading them. I would be thrilled if you've all enjoyed this one.

Now, the acknowledgments.

My editor, as usual, was full of just the right advice that helped make this a better book. You were such a big help with the *Joshi-Ryo* books and now with this one.

To my illustrator, Shiso, thank you for your delicious-looking drawings of pizza and for getting the characters just right! I was invariably excited when the illustrations came and always wanted to see more.

Working with Mushikago Graphics on the design of a book has been a long-standing goal of mine. Yuko Mukadeya and Tetsuya Aoki, thank you for producing such a cute and colorful design.

Finally, to all my readers, my deepest thanks. I hope to see you again.

December 2016
*Kaya Kizaki*

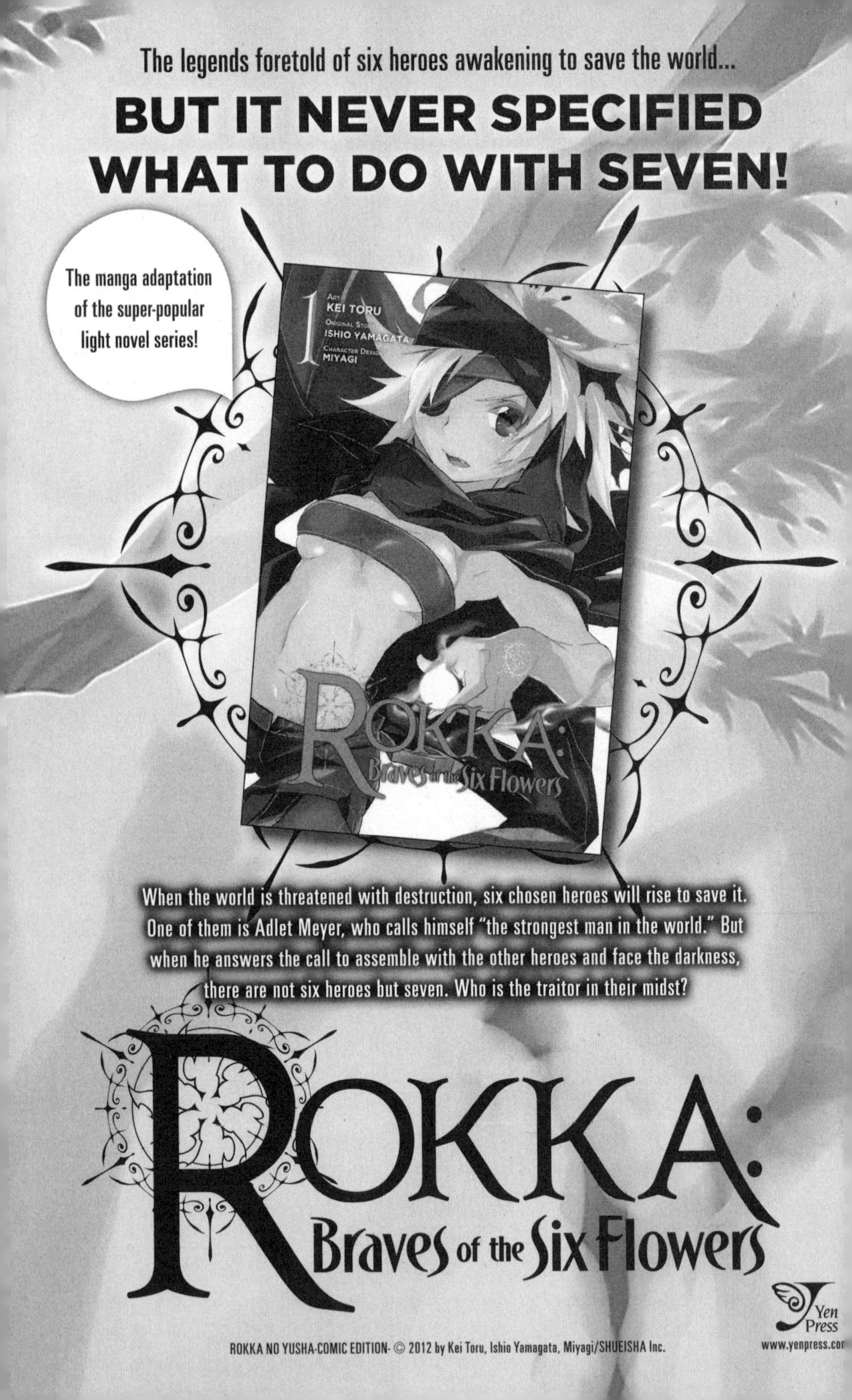
The legends foretold of six heroes awakening to save the world...
BUT IT NEVER SPECIFIED WHAT TO DO WITH SEVEN!
The manga adaptation of the super-popular light novel series!
1
ART: KEI TORU
ORIGINAL STORY: ISHIO YAMAGATA
CHARACTER DESIGN: MIYAGI
ROKKA: Braves of the Six Flowers
When the world is threatened with destruction, six chosen heroes will rise to save it. One of them is Adlet Meyer, who calls himself "the strongest man in the world." But when he answers the call to assemble with the other heroes and face the darkness, there are not six heroes but seven. Who is the traitor in their midst?
ROKKA: Braves of the Six Flowers
Yen Press
ROKKA NO YUSHA-COMIC EDITION- © 2012 by Kei Toru, Ishio Yamagata, Miyagi/SHUEISHA Inc.
www.yenpress.com